He was not the shallow playboy she'd first imagined.

The conviction in his face told her so as he said, "I'm finding I like the clinic and this hospital. And I like my new ranch. So that's a start."

What about a woman to go with all that?

But Nicolette would bite off the end of her tongue before she'd ask him such a thing. She'd be a fool to lose what little heart she had left to a man like him.

She drank her coffee and felt his gaze on her face. His subtle inspection made her extremely aware that she was a woman.

A woman who had not felt the arms of a man around her in years…

Dear Reader,

Each member of the family on the Sandbur ranch has become beloved to me, and when the time came for the oldest daughter to find her soul mate, I wanted him to be a very special man. After all, Nicolette had lost her faith in men and it was going to take more than a charmer with a handsome face and sexy smile to touch her broken heart.

Who was this great guy going to be? The moment Ridge popped into my mind, I liked him. Which was a surprise because normally I'm not attracted to a man like him, who spends his days inside an office— even if his job is saving lives. I'm drawn to strong, outdoor men, whose faces are carved by the elements and with hands callused by hard, honest work. But wait a minute! Ridge isn't just a doctor. At the end of the day he takes off his stethoscope and goes home to pull on his boots. Aaah! What could be sexier than a doctor who wears spurs?

Like me, when Nicolette first meets Ridge, she swoons. But it isn't until she discovers the man inside that she starts to fall in love. He has a mind of his own and values that can't be swayed by money or prestige. He knows exactly what he wants in life— a real marriage, children and a home full of warmth. And he's more than willing to put his family before his career. What woman could resist?

I hope you enjoy reading this latest story in my MEN OF THE WEST series, and please watch for my next book to see how Cordero finally surrenders to love!

Happy trails,

Stella Bagwell

STELLA BAGWELL

THE BEST CATCH IN TEXAS

SPECIAL EDITION®

Published by Silhouette Books

America's Publisher of Contemporary Romance

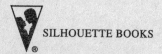

SILHOUETTE BOOKS

ISBN-13: 978-0-373-28062-9
ISBN-10:   0-373-28062-9

THE BEST CATCH IN TEXAS

STELLA BAGWELL

sold her first novel to Silhouette in November 1985. More than fifty novels later, she still loves her job and says she isn't completely content unless she's writing. Recently, she and her husband moved from the hills of Oklahoma to Seadrift, Texas, a sleepy little fishing town located on the coastal bend. Stella says the water, the tropical climate and the seabirds make it a lovely place to let her imagination soar and to put the stories in her head down on paper.

She and her husband have one son, Jason, who lives and teaches high school math in nearby Port Lavaca.

To my dear Marie
and the memory of her beloved Rocky.
Someday you'll be together again.

Chapter One

"Did you get a glimpse of Dr. Garroway's backside? Oooee, what a treat it would be to see him in a pair of jeans."

"Jeans? I'd like to see him without the jeans—without anything—except that smile of his!"

The hushed prattle of the two nurses turned into low giggles just as Nicolette Saddler approached the work desk where stacks of medical charts were waiting to be dispensed to waiting doctors.

"Ladies, do you think one of you might

find the time to dig out Mr. Stanfield's chart?" she asked.

Both women, who were several years younger than Nicolette's thirty-eight years, looked around with shocked, parted lips. Obviously, neither nurse had been aware of her presence as they'd gushed over the new cardiologist.

"Oh!" Embarrassed, one of the nurses whirled toward the pile of manila folders and began to fumble through them. "Oh, sure, Dr. Saddler. Just a moment. It's right here."

Technically, Nicolette wasn't a doctor. She was a P.A., a physician's assistant. But most of her patients and colleagues called her doctor, simply because it was easier.

The second nurse smiled sheepishly. "Uh, we were just discussing the new heart doctor. Everybody in the clinic is excited about him."

Everybody meaning all the women, Nicolette thought, as she did her best to stifle a sigh. From the moment she'd walked into the clinic this morning, she'd heard nothing but praise and adoration for the new cardiologist, who'd filled the empty spot left by Dr. Gray Walters's retirement. But as far as Nicolette was concerned, no man could fill the elderly doctor's shoes. He'd worked tirelessly to see that each and every patient had the best care. While other physicians enjoyed themselves on the golf course, or fishing down on the coast, Dr. Walters had been in the clinic or the hospital, giving of himself to his patients. She didn't expect the same sort of dedication from the new man. From what she'd heard, he was only twenty-nine and the biggest thing he had going for him was his looks.

"Yes, I've heard," Nicolette said drearily. Today was her first day back at Coastal Health since she'd taken two weeks off to nurse her ailing mother. Though she hadn't expected to find Welcome banners for her return, she would have enjoyed having at least one person express their pleasure at seeing her. Instead, the new Dr. Garroway seemed to have turned the place on its ear.

The young nurse looked at her with a puzzled frown. "You don't sound a bit excited. Haven't you met him yet?"

"I'm not excited," Nicolette briskly informed her. "And I haven't met him yet. I have more important things on my agenda. Like sick patients."

She took the chart from the other nurse's hand and left the work station. As she walked down the corridor to her office, she pretty much felt the two women staring after her, as though she was some sort of hardened matron. Maybe they were right, she thought dismally. She couldn't remember the last time she'd gotten excited about a member of the opposite sex. Since she and her ex-husband had parted, she hadn't looked twice at one. She'd had her turn with a good-looking, sweet-talking man and she wasn't interested in having another.

Ten minutes later Nicolette was sitting at her desk, going over a battery of test results before she saw her first patient, when the nurse who worked as her personal assistant stepped through the open doorway.

"There's someone in the waiting room to see you, Doctor," she said.

Frowning, Nicolette glanced up at Jacki, a young woman with a mop of curly red hair and an effervescent smile that lasted throughout the day, even when everyone else was growling with fatigue. For the past three years, Jacki had been at Nicolette's side. She'd become a friend, and thankfully Nicolette could talk to her as such.

"Should be a room full of patients," Nicolette replied dryly.

"The patients are there, plus someone else. I told him I'd see if you had a minute or two."

Nicolette's brows peaked. "Him?"

Nodding, Jacki took a small step into the office, leaned toward Nicolette and whispered loudly, "The new doctor. I think all the women in the waiting area are trying to feign heart trouble."

Murmuring a curse word under her breath, Nicolette tossed down her pen and pushed back her chair. "Why didn't you tell the man I was busy? You certainly wouldn't have been lying!"

Unaffected by Nicolette's sharp words, Jacki made a palms-up gesture. "Because he would only come back later. Besides, he's only trying to be neighborly. Something you normally try to be."

Pressing her lips together, Nicolette rose from the leather desk chair. Jacki was right. Meeting the new doctor in the group was the friendly thing to do. And no one said she had to fawn over the man like the rest of the females at the clinic seemed to be doing. "All right. I'll go meet Dr. Garroway," she said as she swished past the nurse. "And then we'll get to work."

Not pausing to see if Jacki was following, Nicolette strode out of the office and down a narrow hallway. When she pushed through a slatted swinging door and into the waiting room, she saw the back of a tall man standing in the center of a ring of female patients. *Her* patients!

"Oh, hi, Dr. Saddler. You ready to see me?"

The question came from an elderly lady with chronic arthritis whom Nicolette treated on a regular basis. The woman was standing at the far edge of the group and as Nicolette approached the woman, she said, "Hello, Mrs. Gaines, I'll be seeing you in just a few minutes. Right now—"

At that moment Dr. Garroway turned toward Nicolette and for a split second she struggled to keep her jaw from dropping.

From this morning's buzz, she'd expected the man to be young and cute, maybe even handsome. The only thing she'd gotten right was the young part; the rest of him could only be described as striking. At least, she certainly felt as if someone had whammed her right in the diaphragm. Her lungs didn't know whether they wanted to breathe in or out, or simply stop altogether.

Nicolette felt more than saw the people around her move aside as the man stepped toward her. By then she'd collected herself somewhat and offered the new doctor her hand.

"Hello, I'm P.A. Nicolette Saddler," she said. "And you must be Dr. Garroway."

A pair of thin lips pulled back into a wide, crooked smile. "Just Ridge to you, Doctor."

The voice matched the face, she thought. Rough, tough and too sexy to be legal. He was far from the pretty boy she'd expected. He had lean, chiseled features that gave the impression he'd thrown a punch or two in his lifetime. His dark-blond hair was straight, naturally streaked with lighter shades of honey and long enough to be considered shaggy. Even though he'd made an effort to comb it back from his face, a few strands had fallen onto his forehead, giving him an even more rakish look. Warm, whiskey-brown eyes stared out at her beneath a pair of thick, brown brows and the certain gleam in those eyes put her on instant alert.

She cleared her throat as she glanced around at the audience of patients. "Would you like to step back into the hallway for a moment?"

"Sure. Just lead the way."

Taking a deep breath, Nicolette walked back to the swinging door with the doctor right behind her. Once they were inside the corridor she turned to face him, hoping she didn't appear as flustered as she felt.

"I'm sorry about the…nosy patients out there," she apologized. "I just want to say welcome to the clinic."

His lips quirked with amusement while his gaze seemed to dance all over her face. She felt unaccustomed heat rising to her cheeks.

"Don't apologize for the patients," he said. "I like people. Nosy and otherwise. And, though it was nice of you, I actually didn't stop by to receive a welcome. I've been eager to meet you."

Her brows inched upward as she regarded him warily. Why would a doctor like him be interested in meeting a lowly P.A? "Really? I can't imagine why."

He chuckled and the sound skittered over Nicolette's skin like a warm, teasing breeze. She resisted the silly urge to sigh.

He said, "Don't be so modest, Doctor, I hear you're probably the most popular physician in the building. Maybe even in the whole town. I wanted to see for myself just what this superwoman was like."

Embarrassed by his flattery, she glanced away from him. At the end of the hallway, Jacki stood at a work counter that portioned off a small room where medicines were kept. Even though the nurse appeared to be busy, Nicolette suspected she was lingering in hopes of catching a bit of their conversation.

"Someone has obviously been pulling your leg, Dr. Garroway. I'm not even a physician. I'm just an assistant. And as for being popular, that's a real exaggeration."

His tongue clicked with disapproval. "There you go, being modest again. I just walked through your waiting room. It's full. What does that say?"

That she was busy and nothing more, she wanted to tell him. But she bit back the words. It would be highly uncomfortable if she got off on the wrong foot with this man. Especially when the two of them would be working in the same building. But she was getting all sorts of vibes from him and none of them were businesslike.

Trying to keep her voice cool, she said, "It tells me that there're plenty of sick people around here."

Looking back at him, she was jolted once again to find he was studying her intently, as though she were a flower he very much wanted to pluck.

Nicolette breathed deeply and told herself

she was wrong. This young doctor wasn't making eyes at her literally. He was simply being himself—a sexy flirt. These past few days doctoring her mother had worn her down and now her mind must not be turning on the right cog.

"I was told that you used to work under Dr. Walters," he said.

Lord, the man was tall, Nicolette thought. Even though she was five foot eight, she would easily fit under his chin. Not that she would ever get that close, she silently swore. But she had to admit his lean body was a thing of beauty with its wide shoulders, narrow waist and long, muscular legs.

"That's right. Dr. Walters was wonderful. I miss him."

And I wish he were here instead of you. She might as well have said it out loud, Ridge thought, but he didn't let the notion get to him. This woman didn't know him personally. But he was going to make sure that sooner or later she *would*, and maybe then she'd be calling *him* wonderful. He didn't know why changing her mind should be so important to him, especially when he didn't know her personally, either. But all of his colleagues spoke of P.A. Saddler with great admiration. He valued her respect.

"I'm sure you do miss him," he told her. "But Dr. Walters has earned a well-deserved retirement. And I've assured him I'm going to take the best of care of all his patients. He trusts me. Do you?"

She shot him a look that said she considered his question odd. "Trust you?" she repeated skeptically.

He gave her an indulgent smile. "That's right. To be a good, dedicated doctor."

Her gaze lowered to the floor, and Ridge took the moment to study her more closely. From the moment he'd spotted her in the waiting room, he'd found himself wanting to stare. She was nothing like the matronly woman he'd been expecting. Instead of wearing chunky heels, owl-rimmed glasses and a severe bun, she was sporting stiletto heels, clear gray eyes and long brown hair that swung freely to the middle of her back. It would be hard for him to guess her age, but that detail didn't matter. She was the most beautiful, sexy woman he'd ever seen in his life.

"Oh," she said. "Well, I'm sure you know your business. Otherwise you wouldn't be here."

It wasn't the response he wanted to hear from her, and he got the sense that she had already formed an opinion of him. One that wasn't all that flattering.

"I was told you were working with Dr. Kelsey now."

"That's right."

She certainly wasn't helping him with this conversation, he thought. One- or two-word answers didn't tell him much.

"Why?"

Her gray eyes popped wide. "I beg your pardon?"

He shrugged. "I was just wondering why you chose to work with him. Since you worked with Dr. Walters before he retired, I would have thought I'd have been your first choice. Or does dealing with heart ailments bore you?"

It was obvious that his question caught her off guard. She was floundering to come up with the right words.

Clearing her throat, she said, "Dr. Kelsey is a family practitioner. He deals with all sorts of health problems, and I get his overflow. I like the variety. And as for working with you—I don't know you. And no one told me beforehand that you wanted an assistant."

He smiled once again. "I wanted one when I heard about you."

She folded her arms beneath her breasts and Ridge couldn't help but follow the starched fabric of her lab coat as it molded to the rounded mounds. Even with the coat on, he could see she was a shapely woman.

His gaze moved to her left hand, and he was surprised to see it empty of a wedding ring. With her looks he'd figured some man had already branded her a long time ago as his property. But then, she could be a career women who didn't want the extra responsibility of being married, he thought. In any case, finding out more about this woman was on his agenda.

"That's…gracious of you to say, Dr. Garroway, but—"

"I'd really like it if you'd call me Ridge," he interrupted. "After all, I'm sure we'll be running into each other quite often."

Not if she could help it, Nicolette promised herself. The man's charm was as lethal as a flaming arrow and she wasn't about to put herself in the path of the man's aim.

To him she said, "Okay, Ridge it is. But as for us running into each other, I'm sure we're both going to be very busy." She glanced pointedly at her watch. "Which I am right now. I hope you'll excuse me, but I have patients waiting."

She glanced up at him, figuring his expression would have cooled somewhat, but if anything, his smile had deepened and the gleam in his eye was even brighter.

"Of course," he said warmly. "I have work waiting on me, too. But we doctors need to take time out for ourselves, otherwise we'd need somebody to treat us."

To her indignation, he winked and then casually turned to go. Before he pushed through the swinging door, he said over his shoulder, "Nice meeting you, Nicolette."

That night, as Nicolette drove home to the Sandbur Ranch, she couldn't stop thinking about the new Dr. Garroway. In fact, she was angry with herself because he'd popped in and out of her mind all day long. It wasn't like her to be distracted by anyone or anything and she had to admit to herself that she was no better than the nurses who'd been awestruck over the man.

It wasn't as though the man had enthralled her, she argued with herself. No, it was more like he'd irritated her with that cocky grin and that roaming brown gaze. He'd looked at her as though he'd like to eat her. And that wink! It was the most unprofessional thing she'd ever seen. Sexy, true. But totally out of place. Why, the man had only met her minutes before!

Forget it, Nicolette. Forget him, she muttered to herself as she parked her car and gathered her work from the passenger seat. She wasn't going to be working closely with the man. Like she'd told him, she doubted their paths would cross all that much, so it wasn't as if she would be dealing with his brashness on a daily basis.

Now she was ready for a relaxing evening at home. The ranch house where Nicolette lived with her mother and younger brother, Lex, was built in traditional hacienda style with a stucco exterior, a terracotta tile roof and a long ground-level porch with arched supports. The house was huge, as was the other family home on the ranch where her cousins, Matt and Cordero Sanchez, resided.

The Sandbur was not just a little spot near Victoria, Texas. It spread for thousands of acres, and at one time the Saddler and Sanchez families had been large enough to need the spacious houses. At least, when everyone was alive and all the children lived at home the leg room had been needed.

Nowadays things were different. Her younger sister, Mercedes, was presently away serving in the Air Force, and Nicolette's cousin, Lucita, was down in Corpus Christi teaching. As for Nicolette's father, Paul, he'd been laid to rest ten years ago, and nearly six years ago her aunt Elizabeth had passed away from diabetes complications. Even Nicolette had left the ranch for a while during those nine years she'd been married to Bill. But that was another man and another time that Nicolette didn't want to think about.

As she approached the front porch, she saw two bamboo torches shedding a dim, flickering light over someone sitting in a wicker chair. Once she grew close, she could see it was her mother, Geraldine. The woman's feet were propped up on a matching wicker coffee table, and a squatty tumbler was in her hand.

Nicolette released a weary breath.

"Good evening, Nicci. You're very late getting home this evening."

"Hi, Mother." She walked the length of the porch to where her mother sat, then bent to kiss her cheek. "What are you doing outside at this time of night? I told you—"

"Now don't start fussing with me, Nicci," Geraldine interrupted. "I've been cooped up in the house for so long that I'm starting to feel like a nesting hen."

"Better the house than a hospital room," Nicolette reminded her. "And by the way, what is that you're drinking?"

"Cook made me a mild margarita. And believe me, there's not enough tequila in it to make a bird stagger, much less give your old mother a buzz, so quit worrying."

With another heavy sigh, Nicolette sank into a chair positioned at an angle to her mother's. "I guess I sound bossy, don't I? But I just want you to get back to your old self."

For the past two weeks Nicolette's mother had been very ill with an acute case of summer bronchitis. At sixty-three Geraldine still looked young for her age and she was normally strong and healthy, but the summer had been extremely dry and dusty. With Lex and Matteo both busy, she'd taken on the job of overseeing the hay baling in the south meadow. The fog of dust and hay had done a number on her lungs and the only thing that had kept the woman out of the hospital was Nicolette's diligent care.

"I understand that, honey. And you have your right to gripe at me. I caused you to miss two weeks of work. How am I ever going to repay you?"

Nicolette chuckled. Money was not an issue with her or any of her family for that matter. After nearly a century of raising some of the finest beef cattle and cutting horses in the business, the ranch had made both the Saddler and Sanchez families extremely wealthy. Nicolette worked in medicine because she'd always had a deep need to help people, not to make a living.

"Stay out of the hayfield. That's how."

The silver-haired woman held her glass out toward Nicolette. "Have a sip. From the looks of you, you need it."

Nicolette groaned. Her mother didn't have to tell her she looked as tired as dirty dishwater. She'd unfortunately caught a glimpse of herself tonight in the restroom mirror before she'd left the clinic. Her brown hair was fuzzed, dark crescents smudged the skin beneath her eyes, and her skin was pasty with fatigue. If Dr. Ridge Garroway saw her now, she very much doubted he'd give her one of those gleaming smiles. But that didn't matter, she silently insisted. She didn't want one of his smiles or anything else the man had to offer. She wasn't in the market for romance.

"I do need a drink," Nicolette admitted. "I've had a long, long day. Everyone seemed to be ailing with something. Dr. Kelsey couldn't keep up and sent several patients down to my office."

Geraldine reached for the cell phone on the coffee table and began to punch numbers. "Poor darling, put your feet up and I'll call Cook."

Nicolette did as her mother suggested and by the time she got settled, Cook appeared on the porch with a small pitcher of icy margaritas and a glass with a salted rim.

Cook's name was really Hattie Tibideaux, but she'd been the cook for the Sandbur for so many years that everyone simply called her by her profession. Her age had inched beyond seventy now, yet her tall, bony figure was more spry than a woman twenty years younger. In spite of her advanced age, her black hair was only sprinkled with sparse amounts of gray and most often it was pulled severely back from her face in either a ponytail or braid. Her fingernails and lips were always painted red and Nicolette figured the woman had been an exotic beauty in her heyday.

"Thank you, Cook, you're too sweet," Nicolette told her as she placed the pitcher and glass on a small table between the two women.

Cook rose up to her full height and with her hands on her slim hips gave Nicolette a quick survey.

"You look like hell, Miss Nicci. Are they trying to kill you over there at that clinic?"

"Not really. There's just lots of sick folks these days."

The older woman clicked her tongue with disapproval. "Too much hustle and bustle. That's what makes 'em sick. If things were quiet and slow, we'd all live a lot longer."

Nicolette gave the woman a tired smile. "Looks like the fast pace agrees with you, Cook. You don't look a day older than you did ten years ago."

"Hah!" With a loud snort, she waved a dismissive hand at Nicolette and started toward the door. "I don't have a fast pace, Miss Nicci, I stay in the kitchen. Where I'm happy."

The older woman disappeared into the house and Nicolette poured herself a small drink. "I guess that's Cook's secret to good health and longevity. She's happy," she said pensively.

Geraldine looked thoughtfully at her. "Speaking of being happy, there's something on your face tonight, darling, that worries me. Is anything wrong? You're not dwelling on Bill, are you?"

Frowning, Nicolette took a long sip from her glass and glanced out at the wide lawn sloping away from the house. Huge spreading live oaks obstructed the view of the night sky, but between the dipping branches the twinkling lights of her cousin's house could be seen, along with several nightlights skirting the barns and feed lots. For now the ranch was quiet and peaceful and she felt its soothing arms wrap around her weary shoulders.

"If you think I'm still grieving over Bill, you couldn't be more wrong," she said flatly.

Geraldine softly drummed her fingers against the arm of the lawn chair. "You can't deny you were terribly hurt when he left you for that—that other woman."

Nicolette inwardly cringed. Tonight she was hardly in the mood to discuss Bill or her failed marriage, but she didn't want to cut her mother's questions short. Nicolette knew from experience that to do so would only make her mother dig more.

"You know how I feel about that, Mother. It wasn't entirely his fault. I left him alone too many nights and he... decided to stray."

"My Lord, you were working, Nicci! It wasn't like you were out prowling with tom cats while he sat home pining for you."

That much was true, Nicolette thought dismally. But she'd worked incessantly to make herself forget that her husband had misled her, that none of the special plans they'd made before their marriage would ever come true.

"Believe me, none of what Bill did or didn't do matters anymore, Mother."

Geraldine rolled her eyes. "How can you say that when the whole horrible affair is still leading you around by the nose? If it didn't matter, you would have already found yourself another man by now. You'd be married and having kids. Instead, you're still killing yourself trying to doctor half the town!"

Nicolette stiffened with resentment. "Is there anything wrong with that? I thought helping people to be healthy was a noble cause."

"Damn it, Nicci, it *is* noble. But there are

other things to life, you know. I'd like to have grandchildren before I die."

The lonely pain that always lingered in Nicolette's chest throbbed to life. "Lex or Mercedes will give you grandchildren, when the time comes. Besides, you're a long way from dying, Mother."

A disbelieving snort slipped from the older woman as she eyed her eldest child. "I might be a long way from dying, but your brother and sister are even further away from giving me grandchildren. Lex is too much of a playboy to be settling down anytime soon, if ever. And as for Mercedes, she's never going to get over that bastard in college that broke her heart. At least, not enough to marry and have a family."

For some odd reason, the image of Ridge Garroway popped into Nicolette's mind and she wondered if he was a man who would want to settle down and have children. He seemed far from the sort. In fact, with his looks and playful charm, he could have a Nurse Good Body waiting for him in every nook and cranny of the hospital.

Nicolette took another long sip of her drink and hoped the tequila would fuzz the intrusive image of the doctor's impish grin. "Mercedes is in the Air Force, Mother. She has other things on her mind right now. Give her time."

Geraldine slowly shook her head in dismay. "I might as well face the fact that life is different from when I was your age," she muttered. "Back then, young people considered finding a permanent mate an important part of their life."

"It still is important. It's just more difficult for us to do."

As she absently combed fingers through her mussed hair, Nicolette glanced over at her mother. "What in the world has got you off on this subject anyway? It isn't like you to start harping on your children."

Geraldine shrugged with concession. "I wasn't thinking about any of it until you sat down here beside me and I saw your sad face. I thought it might be Bill, but—I guess I was wrong. Want to tell me?"

Nicolette finished off the last of her drink and placed her glass next to the sweaty pitcher. "Don't worry, Mother. I've had a very long day. On top of that I met the doctor who took Dr. Walters's place."

Sudden interest caused Geraldine to sit straight up in her chair. "Oh? How did that go? What was he like?"

It was all Nicolette could do to keep from groaning out loud. "He was—well, to be honest I'm shocked the clinic hired someone so young. I heard he's twenty-nine."

"Being young is hardly a crime," Geraldine pointed out.

Nicolette grimaced. "It means he can't have much experience."

"Everyone has to start at the beginning. You were there once," Geraldine reminded her.

Sighing, Nicolette said, "Yes, I know. But Dr. Walters was so wonderful. And this new man—just doesn't seem that professional to me."

Geraldine's brows arched upward. "Really? What makes you say that?"

With the fingers of both hands, Nicolette massaged her aching forehead. How could she describe that gleam in Ridge Garroway's eyes or that wink he'd given her without throwing for flags at her mother? "He, uh, just doesn't look like a doctor," she said lamely.

Suddenly loud laughter erupted from Geraldine, causing Nicolette to cast an annoying look her mother's way.

"Why are you laughing? It's the truth. He

looked more like some—I don't know—some playboy than a medical person."

Still chuckling, Geraldine asked, "Since when did looks have anything to do with being a doctor? C'mon, Nicci, don't you think you're reaching a little far to find something wrong with the man?"

With thoughtful frown, Nicolette considered her mother's question. *Could Geraldine be right?* she wondered. Had she already planted a seed in her mind to dislike the man before she'd ever met him? Perhaps. But that still didn't account for that flirty attitude of his, she decided.

"Okay, to be honest, I think he's a big flirt. He said all sorts of…suggestive things to me. Like how he wished I'd chosen to work under him rather than Dr. Kelsey."

Geraldine laughed again. "What's wrong with that? I'm sure the man has heard you're good at your job."

Nicolette's lips pursed with disapproval. "Yes, but it was the way he said it that rubbed me all wrong. He had this gleam in his eyes that made me feel like an idiot."

Geraldine placed a gentle hand on her daughter's arm. "Don't you mean it made you feel like a woman?"

Her mother's suggestion left Nicolette so uncomfortable she quickly jumped to her feet and snatched up the briefcase she'd propped against the legs of her chair.

"I'm going to go take a shower and have a little supper," she told her mother. "It's getting late and I've got to be at the clinic very early in the morning."

Chapter Two

A few minutes later, after showering and dressing in a robe, Nicolette was almost too tired to eat the plate of food Cook set in front of her. But eventually she managed to swallow down half of the broiled salmon and rice before she headed to her bedroom.

She'd brought home several journal articles about new medications soon to be released, but as soon as she crawled into bed and picked up the first one, her eyelids began to droop.

Two hours later she was sound asleep with the lamp on the nightstand still burning, when the telephone jangled loudly near her head. Since she had a private line she couldn't rely on Cook or her mother to answer.

Trying to shake away her grogginess, she reached for the phone and shoved her hair back from her face.

"Hello."

"Is that you Ms. Saddler? Nicolette, isn't it?"

The voice sounded vaguely familiar but she couldn't quite put a name to it. "Yes. Who is this?"

"Dr. Garroway—Ridge—remember?"

In spite of her numbing exhaustion, Nicolette shot straight up in the bed and gripped the receiver. "Doctor. Uh, why are you calling? It's—" Twisting her head around toward the digital clock on the nightstand, she was shocked to see it was twenty minutes past midnight. "It's very late. And—"

"I'm sorry to wake you like this, Nicolette, but I'm having a little problem here at the hospital and—"

His use of her first name distracted her even more and she blurted out with surprise, "You're at the hospital?"

"Uh, yes. I am a doctor," he reminded dryly.

She felt desperately stupid as she tried to wake herself up and gather her scattered senses. "Sorry. I'm not—I was sound asleep. You say you're having a problem? What does that have to do with me?"

There was a moment's pause and then he said, "My patient is demanding to see you. Seems you're his favorite doctor and he won't trust me to treat him unless you're here. I tried to explain—"

"Who's the patient?" Nicolette interrupted him again.

"Dan Nelson. He's—"

Dan Nelson was ninety-one years old and had worked as a wrangler for the Sandbur until he was in his mideighties. He was a prickly pear of an old man, but she adored him. "Yes, yes, I know the man. I'll be there in twenty minutes."

"Wait, Nicolette. Driving to the hospital might not be necessary. Talking to him over the phone might work," Ridge told her.

"He's more important to me than that," she said curtly.

There was another short pause and then he said, "All right, I appreciate your help. And by the way, I'm at the county hospital."

"I'll find you."

Nicolette dropped the phone on its hook and scurried from the bed.

As she hastily grabbed clothes from the closet, she groaned out loud. Meeting Ridge Garroway in the middle of the night was the last thing she wanted to do. But Dan needed her and she was a medical provider first, a woman second.

As long as she could keep that fact in the back of her mind, she could meet the new doctor head-on and never suffer the slightest heart murmur.

Twenty minutes later Nicolette wheeled her car into the hospital parking lot and hurried inside. At the double elevators, she smashed the up button, and as she waited for a door to open, she hurriedly jerked a white lab coat over her shirt and jeans and fastened the buttons.

Once she reached the third floor, where most of the internal medicine patients were located, she hurried toward the nurses' station, where several women were clustered behind a tall counter.

Bess, an older nurse sitting at a computer located directly behind the counter, looked up at Nicolette with faint surprise. "P.A. Saddler, is that you?"

Nicolette unconsciously lifted a hand to her long hair. She'd not taken the time to fasten it with a barrette or even a rubber band and now it was flying around her shoulders. Her face was bare of makeup and she realized she must look very pale and very unprofessional, but her appearance was the last thing she was worried about at the moment.

"It's me, Bess, I'm looking for Dr. Garroway. Is he on the floor?"

Bess nodded. "Last I saw he was down at room 301 with a Mr.—" she glanced at a clipboard with a list of patients' names "—Mr. Nelson."

"Thanks."

From the nurses' station Nicolette made a quick turn to the left, which would take her down an east wing. She was almost to the private room when Dr. Garroway suddenly stepped out in the corridor.

He smiled and waved. Nicolette swallowed hard and hurried toward him.

"How is he?" she asked before he had a chance to say a word.

The apprehension on her face caused the doctor's brows to lift. "Are you close to Mr. Nelson?"

"I've known him since I was a very small

girl. He worked for my family for more than fifty years. Of course I'm close to him. I love him."

He placed a hand on her shoulder. Nicolette had not been asking for any comfort from the man, but she realized the strength of his touch was very steadying and, at the moment, very welcome.

"Relax. I think Mr. Nelson is going to be fine. That is, if he'll allow me to treat him. He needs a shot of diuretics to reduce the fluid in his lungs, but he won't agree to let me or the nurse give it to him."

A sigh of relief rushed past Nicolette's lips. "I know his heart isn't the best in the world. I was afraid he'd suffered an attack."

"No. Nothing like that. Right now this is mainly a pulmonary problem."

Nodding that she understood, Nicolette grimaced. "Years of unfiltered cigarettes," she explained, then added, "I'll see what I can do. He's usually good for me."

"I'd appreciate that," Ridge said, then gestured toward the closed door.

Nicolette knocked lightly and stepped into the small room. One fluorescent light burned over the head of Dan's bed, illuminating the older man's wrinkled face. At the moment, his faded blue eyes were closed, but when she spoke they flew wide open.

"Dan? It's me, Nicci," she said softly. "How are you feeling?"

He held his hand out to her and motioned her to his side. Nicci hurried to him and clasped the bony hand between hers.

"Nicci, honey, I thought you'd never get here."

She rubbed his arm and then passed her fingers over his damp forehead. "Well, I'm here now. Tell me what's wrong."

"Nothin's wrong! I'm just havin' a little trouble breathin'. That damned old woman who thinks she's my keeper thought I needed to come to the hospital. I've already told her I'm gonna fire her for this," he muttered. "All I need is a good shot of bourbon. But she wouldn't give it to me!"

In spite of the situation, Nicci had to hide her smile. "You're talking about Opal? The lady that keeps house for you?"

"That's her. Nosiest female I've ever seen." He snorted, then pointed over her shoulder to where Ridge stood just inside the door. "And that young whippersnapper over there wants to jab me with a needle. He don't know what I need. He's still wet behind the ears!"

Nicolette rubbed her hand gently across Dan's chest. "Dan, Doctor Garroway is trying to help you. And he does know what he's doing. The shot will help your lungs."

"Hmmp. Well, that stuff will make me go to the bathroom all night long. Nope—I won't take it."

The old man stubbornly shook his head, and Nicolette turned a stern look on him. "You will take it or I'll get Mother in here after you," she warned. "And you know she won't be nearly as sweet with you as I'm being."

He studied her through squinted eyes, then gave her a weak grin. "Honey child, you always were my little sweetheart. I guess if you say I need the shot, then I'll just have to take it. I won't like it, mind you, but I'll take it. For you."

"That's my guy," she said happily, then leaned down and kissed his forehead. "I want you to get well. That's why you're going to do everything Dr. Garroway tells you. Okay?"

He nodded and she placed one last kiss on his cheek before she straightened to her full height and motioned for Ridge to join her.

"If you have the diuretic with you, I'll give it to him," she told the doctor.

"The nurse took it back to the station." He

picked up the call button and quickly ordered the medicine back to Dan's room. Once the RN returned with the prepared shot, Ridge instructed her to leave it with Nicolette.

Quickly, before the old wrangler had a change of heart, Nicolette injected him with the medicine and promised him she would be just outside the door if he needed her.

She and Dr. Garroway left the room and walked a short distance down the hall. Since it was long past regular visiting hours, the lights in the corridor had been dimmed and the hospital wing was quiet. Once they were far enough away from Dan's door, Ridge paused and turned a grateful look on her.

"Thank you, Nicolette, for all this trouble you've taken. It's ruined your night and I feel badly about that. But Mr. Nelson will get well much more quickly now. I could have badgered him into taking the shot, but I didn't want to put added stress on the man. And I'm not too proud to ask for help when help is needed," he added with a grin.

Apparently not, Nicolette thought, and the fact surprised her very much indeed. She'd figured that at his age, he would be a doctor who thought he walked on water and never needed help from anyone, especially from a mere physician's assistant. It was nice to learn she'd been wrong.

"Don't worry about it," she assured him. "Dan pretends to be grouchy, but he really has a heart as soft as a marshmallow. I don't think he'll give you any more problems about medication now."

He smiled, and even in the semidarkness, Nicolette could feel the punch of his charm. There was something sparkling and vibrant about the man, as though he loved life and wanted everyone around him to do the same.

"Actually the old man is in good shape for his age. He may eventually need a pacemaker, but we'll deal with that when the time comes. Uh, you say he worked for your family...what did he do?"

Apparently he either didn't know about the Sandbur or he didn't associate her with the families who ran it. The idea that he was unaware she was a rich, ranching heiress was rather nice.

"Ranch wrangler. You couldn't find a better cowboy in Texas. He's spent more hours in the saddle than you've been alive," Nicolette told him.

His brows lifted and he chuckled. "Come on now, pretty lady, I'm not *that* young."

And she wasn't supposed to be a pretty lady. At least not to him. He was a professional, a colleague; he should be behaving appropriately.

"Dan might argue that point," she said briskly, then glanced pointedly at her watch. "I think I'll go down to the cafeteria and wait around until the diuretic takes affect, just to make sure he begins to improve."

A grin dimpled Ridge's cheeks. "You can go on home and go to bed, Nicolette. I'll make sure Mr. Nelson is taken care of."

She was exhausted and needed to be resting, but she knew if she went home now she'd only toss worriedly in her bed. Doctors like him made diagnoses, ordered medicines and left the rest up to the nurses while they went on their merry way.

Nicolette started walking toward the nearest elevator. "The nurses here are good, but I want to check on him myself."

He strode along beside her and Nicolette was intensely aware of his tall, muscular frame only inches from her and the faint masculine cologne drifting to her nostrils. For that one brief moment, she realized with a measure of disgust, she was no different from the nurses at the clinic; she would love to see all those hard muscles that must be hidden by his shirt and chinos.

"Nurses. What about me?" he asked.

Surprise caused Nicolette to miss a step. "Aren't you going home now?"

He looked at her with disappointment. "You really don't think much of me, do you?"

Whipping her attention to the end of the corridor, she grimaced. "I expect you're going to have a busy practice, Dr. Garroway. You can't stay up all night at the hospital and expect to give them expert care."

"Well, I'm glad to hear that you understand I'm human. Young, but human," he said teasingly.

From the corner of her eye, she could see that he was smiling again. Obviously, he was not a man who angered easily. Another positive in his corner, she thought, and wondered why the fact only irritated her.

By now they'd reached the nurses' station. To the left of the long counter was an elevator. Nicolette could see Bess eyeing the two of them as they waited for the door to open. No doubt the old nurse was wondering what the new cardiologist was doing stuck to Nicolette's side. Tomorrow there would probably be rumors about them all over the hospital, she thought grimly. Oh well, it wouldn't be the first time she'd been discussed among the nurses. She didn't date or socialize with the staff and she kept her personal life to herself. Nicolette realized that that in itself made her fodder for gossip.

In the elevator, Ridge stood at Nicolette's shoulder and covertly studied her appearance. He'd been surprised, no shocked was more like it, when he'd spotted her flying up the hallway toward Dan Nelson's room. Even though she was wearing a starched prim lab coat with her name embroidered across the left breast, he could easily see that underneath she was wearing jeans and cowboy boots. Her long shiny hair had been flying loose around her head and she'd looked like a different woman from the staunch professional she'd projected this morning. She'd looked as sexy as hell in a dress and high heels, but she was even more attractive like this. With her beautiful face bare of makeup and her hair tousled, she looked like a sensual, touchable woman. And Ridge realized he very much wanted to touch.

"You have patients on the bottom floor?" she asked, when he didn't punch a different floor.

"No. I'm going with you to the cafeteria. That is, if you don't mind," he added slyly.

She looked at him with arched brows. "Why?"

One corner of his mouth curled upward. "Because I need to kill some time while the medication works on Mr. Nelson. And I thought you'd be good company."

Her lips pressed together. Now was the time to discourage him, she told herself, to get across to him that men, even one like him, weren't a part of her life. "I'm not good company at anytime, much less in the middle of the night. You'd be better off going back up and visiting with Bess while you wait."

"Bess doesn't intrigue me."

Her head jerked up and an annoyed scowl wrinkled her forehead. "Look—uh, Ridge, I'm not interested in your…flirting!"

He raised his palms in an innocent gesture. "Flirting! Who said I was flirting? I was merely making a statement that I find you more interesting than Bess. And far more attractive."

She should have been angry with him for being so forward, but instead her heart thumped at the idea that he found her attractive. She'd not thought of herself in that way for years and now a very young man like him taking a second look at her was very flattering.

"Is this the way you behave with all female doctors?"

"You're a physician's assistant." His smile was broad and just wicked enough to send a spurt of color to her cheeks. "Actually, no," he added. "You seem to be doing something to me."

The door to the elevator slid open. As Nicolette stepped out, she said over her shoulder, "Then you'd better make a quick diagnosis and treat yourself."

Chuckling, he quickly caught up to her as she stalked down a hallway that led to the cafeteria. "Nicolette, you can make a joke! I'm surprised!"

Knowing she was enjoying this banter with him too much, she stopped and whirled toward him. "Look, for your information, I didn't drive to the hospital in the middle of the night just to be your—company! I'm only here because of Dan."

He appeared to be offended. A frown of irritation creased his forehead and twisted his lips. "I didn't ask you here for your company. Since we have the same goal, I thought sharing a few minutes would be the natural thing to do."

Her eyes widened. "Goal?" she asked inanely.

"Yes. Mr. Nelson's well-being. That is why we're both here, isn't it?"

Nicolette felt like an idiot and she looked away from him as she tried to gather her thoughts. She didn't know what it was about this man, but he had the ability to make her feel about sixteen years old.

Drawing in a deep breath, she glanced up at him. "Sorry. I-I'm rather tired and edgy tonight. Please, join me in the cafeteria?"

He smiled then and cupped his hand around her elbow, urging her toward the dining area. "I'd be delighted. Although, I'm afraid everything looks closed at this hour."

"We can use the vending machines," she told him. "And the coffeepot should be going."

"Sounds good enough to me."

They walked to the machines and loaded them with what change they had between them. Ridge purchased a sandwich and Nicolette settled for a package of cheese and crackers. They added foam cups of coffee to the food, then found a small round table near a wall of plate glass.

Except for the two of them, the dining area was empty and so quiet Nicolette could practically hear her own heart pounding in her ears. As she tore into the package of crackers, she told herself she was reacting to the man in a juvenile way. If she were smart, she would treat his flirting with indifference and give him the message that he wasn't affecting her in the slightest way. But she'd never been a good actress.

Across from her, Ridge bit into the roast beef sandwich and grimaced at its dryness. "Not the best in the world, but at least it's filling."

"Did you eat dinner tonight?"

He shook his head. "I had two emergencies earlier this evening. Once I took care of them I drove home and had barely gotten in the house when the phone rang again. That call was Mr. Nelson, and I've been dealing with him ever since."

Nicolette suddenly felt very guilty for thinking he would be one of those doctors who called in orders and expected the nurses to care for his patients. Maybe she had misjudged him, especially about his dedication to his patients. Yet she was sure she hadn't misconstrued his brashness. He'd probably learned to charm women even before he headed to kindergarten.

"Sounds like you're getting off to a busy start. You might wish you'd never moved to this area," she suggested.

He shook his head. "I won't do that. I really like it around here. I've already bought a place west of the city. Busy or not, this is where my roots are sinking."

Curious, she studied him as he wolfed down the sandwich. "Do you have family in the area?"

He reached for his coffee. "No. They're all in Houston."

"You didn't want to practice there?"

To Nicolette's surprise a bland mask covered his face. Maybe everything in his life wasn't as cheery as he projected.

"I've lived in Houston all my life. My parents and grandparents are still there. But now that I'm out of medical school and practicing, I couldn't get out of there fast enough."

She leaned back in her chair as she nibbled on a cracker. "Why is that? Or is that question too personal? If it is, you don't have to answer."

One of his shoulders lifted and fell. "I don't mind telling you. The place was too big and fast. I don't want to spend my life like a hamster racing uselessly on a wheel."

For the first time since Nicolette had met him, his eyes were solemn, maybe even sad, and the sight touched her in a way that surprised her. She wanted to know more about him. She wanted to understand him. She suddenly cared whether he was happy or sad. And that was dangerous.

"Is that what you thought? That your life there was useless?"

A corner of his mouth lifted faintly. "No. I've had a nice life, a fine education. But I never planned to stay there. From the time I was a young boy, I knew I wanted something different for myself."

"You mean different from your parents and grandparents?"

He nodded. "My father and grandfather are both doctors, too. In fact, my father still has a practice there. He's a neurologist. Gramps was a general practitioner, back in the days when those were still used," he added wryly.

"So you became a heart doctor. That's how you wanted to be different?"

"No. I didn't want to build a practice in Houston. I wanted my life to be—" Grimacing, he paused, swallowed some coffee, then placed the cup down on the tabletop. "I didn't want to live like my father and grand-father, Nicolette. They were both consumed with their jobs and consumed with all the social things that went with living in a huge city. There's life beyond medicine, you know, and I want one. A life that means something."

The conviction on his face struck her and she suddenly realized that he was not the shallow playboy she'd first imagined.

"And you think you can find that here?" she quietly questioned.

A wry grin exposed a portion of his white teeth. "I'm going to try my best. At least I'm finding I like the clinic and this hospital. And I like my new place. So that's a start."

And what about a woman to go with it, Nicolette wondered. But she'd bite the end of her tongue off before she'd ask him such a thing. It didn't matter to her if he had a steady love interest. She'd had her turn with love and marriage, and the experience had left her spirit bound with scars. She'd be a fool to lose what little heart she had left to a man like him.

She drank a portion of her strong coffee while she felt his gaze roaming over her face and hair, touching her lips and lingering on her breasts. His subtle inspection made her extremely aware that she was a woman, a woman who'd not felt the arms of a man around her in years.

Resisting the urge to squirm, she asked, "Uh, did you buy acreage?"

"Two hundred acres. Not very much, but enough for five horses and a small herd of cattle."

Her jaw dropped. "Livestock? You own livestock?"

He chuckled at the stunned look on her face. "That's right. I've always wanted to do a little ranching and now I have the chance. True, I won't have a lot of free time for it. But I'll make the most of what I have."

"What about the golfing, the boating and fishing? And traveling?"

Chuckling, he held up a hand to stem her questions. "Nicolette, where did you get this stereotype of doctors? We're not all made from the same mold, you know."

He was right, of course. But from the moment she'd spotted him standing in her waiting room this morning, maybe even before that, she'd formed her own ideas of the man. Now she was learning he was nothing as she'd first imagined. The fact left her shaken. It only proved that she was no better a judge of men now than she had been when she'd married Bill and believed all his hogwash.

"Sorry. But that's what most of the doctors around here do with their free time. Not that's there anything wrong with golfing or fishing. I just thought—" She paused and shrugged one shoulder. "Well, I've lived nearly all my life on a ranch and you—just don't seem the type."

This time he looked at her with surprise. "You live on a ranch?"

She nodded. "The Sandbur. It's—"

"The Sandbur!" he exclaimed. "*You* are one of *those* Saddlers?"

"You know of the place?"

Leaning back in his chair, he studied her as though the revelation called for him to inspect her all over again. "Of course I know of it! It's spoken in the same breath as the Four Sixes, the Johnson, and the King—"

"Whoa," she interrupted, "don't put us in the same categories as those great Texas ranches, especially the King. We're big, but nothing close to being *that* big."

Her remark didn't seem to dim his respect. "Hmm. Fancy that. You live on the Sandbur. That's exciting. Really exciting."

She crumpled the empty cellophane that

had held the crackers and cheese. "I don't know about exciting. It's just home to me. I live with my mother and brother."

"No husband?"

Unconsciously, her eyes turned to flint as she glanced his way. "No. I'm divorced."

"Oh. Sorry. Guess that really wasn't my business, but I was curious," he admitted.

Her nostrils flared, and Ridge realized he'd touched on a very raw spot. But from the moment he'd met her this morning, he'd been craving more information about the woman. Since she was absent a wedding ring, he'd pretty much decided she wasn't married. But at her age, there had to be a reason for her being single. He'd been tempted to ask some of the clinic nurses about her. But he'd stopped himself from going that far.

"It's nothing secret," she said. "Most everyone knows that's why I moved back to the Sandbur. San Antonio didn't hold much charm for me after Bill and I divorced."

He desperately wanted to ask her what had happened to ruin her marriage. But he didn't. She was just now letting down that defensive cloak she wore tightly around her. He didn't want to push his luck.

"Sorry, Nicolette," he said again. "You,

uh, don't think things will ever work out for you two?"

She stared at him, then let out a brittle laugh. "Not hardly. He's married again. You see, I was…getting a little too old for him," she added. She tossed the crumpled cellophane into her coffee cup and rose to her feet. "I think I'll go back to Dan's room."

Following her example, he gathered up his trash and rose from the plastic chair. "I'll go with you. Hopefully the diuretic has been working."

After disposing of the remains of their snack, the two of them left the cafeteria and headed back to the elevator. Neither of them spoke until they reached the old wrangler's room.

"I'll stay out here in the hall until you finish examining him," Nicolette said.

He frowned at her. "Don't be silly. You're my colleague. Besides, Mr. Nelson will feel more comfortable with you by my side."

She couldn't argue that point, so she nodded and followed him into the room.

Dan was asleep, which was a good sign that his breathing had eased. But as they approached the narrow bed, the old man opened his eyes.

"Well, I can see there's nothing wrong

with your ears," Ridge told the man. He checked the patient's feet and ankles for swelling, then pulled the end of his stethoscope out of his lab coat pocket and warmed it with his hand. "How are you feeling now? Breathing a bit easier?"

Dan nodded, and though he kept a skeptical eye on the new doctor, he didn't complain when Ridge leaned over him and placed the instrument against his chest.

"I'm feelin' better," he said. "Just tired of gettin' in and out of this bed to use the toilet."

"Well, the medicine will wear off in a few hours and then you can get some good sleep. I might even let you go home in a few hours—that is if you behave yourself. Now raise up and breathe deeply for me," he instructed.

Dan sat up in the bed, and Ridge listened carefully. After a moment he looked over to Nicolette and motioned for her to join him.

"Have a listen."

Surprised at his generosity, she took the stethoscope and carefully listened to Dan's heart and lungs. What she heard put a small smile on her face.

"Sounds pretty good," she said. "I think he's on the mend."

The old man snorted. "I ain't sick enough to need two doctors!"

"That's why I'm going home," Nicolette told him, then leaned across the bed railing and kissed his grizzled cheek. "Mind Dr. Garroway, you hear? And I'll see you tomorrow."

He nodded, and Nicolette left the room with Ridge right behind her. Before she had a chance to walk away, he caught her by the arm.

"I just wanted to thank you again, Nicolette. You've made this whole night easy for me. And enjoyable."

There was no flirtatious light in his eyes now; only warm sincerity, and Nicolette found that idea even harder to deal with.

She looked down and away from his brown eyes. "It's no problem. I'm just glad Dan is improving."

"I'll probably release him around noon. Before that, I'm going to put him on medication that will hopefully keep this sort of incident from happening again. I don't know if he'll agree to have regular checkups in the future. Maybe you can help me on that count."

"I'll do my best," she said. Lifting her eyes back to his, she did her best to give him a friendly smile. "You'd better wind your night up, too, and rest before morning comes. See ya around, Doctor."

Nicolette walked away before he could make any sort of reply, but she could feel him watching her walk down the dimly lit corridor. It was a great relief when she was finally able to turn the corner and step into the elevator.

Chapter Three

The next morning when Jacki entered Nicolette's office, she paused at the corner of her boss's desk and sniffed with appreciation.

"Mmm. Something smells delicious." Spotting a flat box with ribbon tied around it, the red-haired nurse picked it up and sniffed at the white cardboard. "It's in here. What is it? May I have some?"

"It's Cook's famous pecan and chocolate chip cookies. And no you can't have one. Neither can I. She's sending them to Dan."

Jacki smiled slyly as she placed the box

back on the desk. "Oooh. Do I smell romance along with the cookies?"

Nicolette finished the last notation on the medical chart in front of her before she looked up at Jacki. "Cook has known Dan for many years. She calls him an old codger, but I think she has a soft spot for him. As for romance, I doubt it. Since her husband was killed in the Viet Nam war, she hasn't shown too much interest in men. Besides, she's in her early seventies now."

"So what? A woman's never too old for romance. Did *you* ever think about that?" Jacki asked pointedly.

Hoping her expression was vacant, Nicolette closed the chart and handed it to her nurse. "I don't consider myself too old for romance, Jacki. I'm just not interested."

Jacki shook her head shook in disbelief. "Why not? Just because your husband was a—"

"I don't want to hear it," Nicolette said firmly. "What is this, anyway? First my mother and now you start in on me about being single. Is something floating around in the air?"

"As far as I'm concerned, it's not about you being single. It's about you being alone."

Rolling her eyes, Nicolette leaned back in the desk chair and gestured at the pile of medical charts on her desk. "I'm hardly alone, Jacki. I'm with people from the time I get up to the time I go to bed."

Jacki shot her a droll look. "It's not the same and we both know it."

Jacki was right. It wasn't the same, Nicolette thought. But it was better than being deceived and manipulated and stomped on by a man.

"I'm happy as I am, Jacki. Let's leave it at that. Now, how many patients do I have left before lunch break? I need to take these cookies over to the hospital to Dan before Dr. Garroway releases him."

"There are two. Mr. Mayfield and Mrs. Gates."

Nicolette rose from her chair and straightened her lab coat. "Good. Let's deal with them and then we'll break for lunch."

She left the room and Jacki followed closely on her heels. "Uh, Nicci, you haven't told me what happened last night with Dr. Garroway. You only said he called you for help."

Nicolette had been trying her best to put last night out of her mind, but so far she'd made little progress. From the moment she'd crawled out of bed, she'd thought about the new doctor and all the things he'd said to her. Even the brief moments he'd touched her seemed to be etched in her memory, playing over and over like an unwanted song.

"Nothing happened last night. I talked Dan into taking his medicine. Dr. Garroway thanked me for my help. That pretty much sums up the whole thing."

Jacki threw up her hands as the two women headed for the nearest examining room. "But you must have talked to the man! What was he like? Did you learn anything about him?"

Nicolette paused to toss an impatient look of warning at the nurse. "Yes. I learned he's not quite what he appears to be."

Jacki opened her mouth to press for more, but Nicolette didn't give her the chance. After knocking lightly on the examining room door, she stepped inside and went to work.

It was ten minutes until noon before Nicolette finally managed to leave the clinic and head to the hospital. She half expected to find Dan gone, but the older man was still there, dressed and sitting on the side of the bed.

He gave Nicolette a broad smile as she kissed his cheek.

"You look much better today," she said with genuine joy and then teased, "Are you ready to leave this place? Or would you like to stay a little longer?"

"Don't press me, girl. I've had all of this pokin' and proddin' that I can stand."

She chuckled. "Now you know how those cows feel when you vaccinate and brand them and cut off their horns." She placed the box of cookies next to him. "Looks like Dr. Garroway has you on the mend. Are you taking your medicine like he says?"

Dan nodded and leaned his head thoughtfully to one side. "Yep. I don't like it, but I guess I can do it. You know that young doctor ain't too bad after all. He says he has some cows and horses and wants me to take a look at 'em for him. Guess the whippersnapper knows where to come to for advice. I've decided to trust him—unless he does somethin' to change my mind."

So the new doctor had charmed Dan, Nicolette thought with surprise. The old wrangler was a tough character. If Ridge could win him over, then she needed to be on guard.

Nicolette gestured to the box of cookies.

"Cook sent you a little get-well gift. Maybe when you get home you ought to call her and thank her."

The old man turned a suspicious eye on the box. "What the hell did she do that for? She knows I don't like her."

Nicolette shook a shaming finger at him. "Don't be lying, Dan."

His expression suddenly sheepish, Dan shifted on the edge of the mattress. "Well, maybe that wasn't the truth. But the old woman…makes me uncomfortable."

Nicolette tried not to smile at the idea of Dan calling someone twenty years his junior old. And then she suddenly thought of Jacki's comments that women were never too old for romance. Maybe the same held true for men.

She cast him a sly glance. "Cook's pretty and she gets you stirred up. That's closer to the truth, isn't it?"

Dan pursed his lips as though he was going to argue, but then he suddenly let out a deep chuckle. "Well, old Hattie is some looker."

They were both still laughing at his admission when a nurse arrived with a wheelchair to take him downstairs. Nicolette placed the box of cookies on his lap and walked along with him. Outside, he climbed spryly into the vehicle with his housekeeper, and Nicolette promised to see him soon, then waved the two of them off.

Moments later she was walking across the parking lot toward her car when someone from behind called out her name.

"Nicolette! Wait up!"

She recognized his voice even before she turned to see Ridge Garroway hurrying toward her. The sight of him in dark slacks and a gray-and-white-striped shirt was enough to make her stare and wish, just for a moment, that she had a whole and trusting heart.

"Hello, Ridge," she said when he finally reached her.

Grinning, he swiped a hand at the blond hair blowing across his forehead. "Been seeing Dan off?"

She nodded. "I was glad he was looking so much better."

His eyes roamed her face with appreciation. "I'm glad to see you looking more rested."

And she was glad to be seeing him again. It was an awful admission, even if she was only making it to herself.

Feeling awkward now, she glanced pointedly at her watch. "Well, I only have a short time left for lunch. I'd better be going."

"That's why I called out to you," Ridge told her. "I'm on my way to lunch, too. I'd like it very much if you'd join me."

Oh no. It would be risky, even foolish to spend one moment more in this man's company than was necessary. On the other hand, when exactly had she turned into such a coward? Ridge Garroway couldn't eat her. He couldn't hurt her. Not unless she allowed him to. And she was a grown woman. She had more sense than to let him get that close.

Before she could change her mind, she blurted out, "Well, if you're inviting, I suppose I could. This once."

"Great!" He said and quickly reached for her arm. "My truck is right over here."

The June day was already hot, with a humid breeze whipping from the southeast. The wind was picking at the fluttery pink hem of Nicolette's skirt and threatening to toss it over her head. She held it down firmly with one hand as Ridge helped her into the passenger seat of his red Ford truck.

"Do you have a favorite eating place?" he asked as he buckled his seat belt and started the engine.

Nicolette looked at him blankly. How could she think of restaurants when he was sitting so close beside her, his blond hair mussed, a sexy smile dimpling his cheeks? He was enough to turn a woman's senses upside down.

"No. Just go wherever you were planning to go. I'm not a picky eater."

"All right, we'll be there in less than two minutes."

The lunch hour traffic was heavy on the main thoroughfares, but they traveled less than two blocks before Ridge turned onto a side street and parked in front of an older wooden building painted a dull turquoise trimmed in pink.

"This is one of the best Mexican restaurants I've found in the whole town. Okay with you?"

"Fine," she said, while asking herself how she'd ended up here with the very man she'd planned to avoid. She shouldn't have been so impulsive, she thought with a bit of self-disgust. She should have gone back to the clinic and eaten a sandwich at her desk. But in spite of what she'd told Jacki, she was tired of being alone. And Ridge Garroway made her feel alive. More alive than she'd felt in years.

He helped her out of the truck, then kept

his hand at her back as he ushered her into the little restaurant. Her flowered blouse was made of thin voile and she could feel the heat of his fingers spreading up and down her spine as they walked to a vacant booth in the back of the room.

The plate-glass windows on the west side of the building were covered with woven shades to block out the hot sun and leave the dining room cool and dimly lit. It took Nicolette's eyes a few moments to adjust as they seated themselves and waited for someone to bring menus.

"You eat a lot of Mexican food?" she asked.

"Actually, I eat too much of it. It's my favorite. So I try to exercise more to keep the calories and the cholesterol in check."

She smiled faintly. "What a novelty, a doctor who tries to practice what he preaches."

His eyes glided over the part of her that wasn't hidden beneath the tabletop. "You look like you keep in great shape. Do you go to the gym?"

Nicolette wrinkled her nose with distaste. "Never. I don't like gyms. I think natural exercise is the best. So I ride horses whenever I can. And I walk as much as possible."

"You know, I've got to confess that last night at the hospital, I wondered why you showed up in jeans and boots. It's not usual attire for women in the medical profession."

A wry smile touched her lips. "Sorry. Those were the most available things in my closet and I was in a hurry. I didn't mean to offend you."

He tilted his head back and laughed. "I wasn't offended, Nicolette. I was intrigued. And by the way," he added, as he settled a twinkling gaze back on her face, "you looked as sexy as hell."

Heat poured into her cheeks and she cleared her throat with plans to remind him not to get so personal. But the waitress appeared before she had a chance to say anything and for the next few moments the two of them were busy choosing drinks and food.

Once the waitress was gone, he said, "I think you'll be glad to hear that Mr. Nelson has agreed to take his daily medication and come in for routine checkups. Hopefully I can keep him on the right track."

Nicolette sipped from a glass of water the waitress had left behind. "He told me that you want him to take a look at his livestock. That was a nice gesture. It made him feel important. Now that his wife has passed on, the man doesn't have anyone, except for his housekeeper."

"I wasn't doing it just to make him feel important," he said. "He has years of experience and knowledge with cattle and horses. I would value his opinion and advice and be glad to pay him for it."

Once again he'd revealed that he wasn't above asking for help. Apparently he wasn't one of those guys that thought he knew more than everyone else on every subject under the sun the way her ex-husband had. During their marriage, Bill had worked as an executive for an insurance firm in San Antonio and he'd been good at his job. Yet the man had been hopelessly lacking with manual tasks of any kind. Even so, he'd found it offensive if she'd suggested he get help from a mechanic for an ailing car, or a plumber to replace a leaky faucet.

"I'm sure Dan will be more than glad to help you," Nicolette commented.

He started to make some sort of reply when he suddenly frowned and reached to his shirt pocket for his vibrating cell phone.

"Excuse me," he said as he flipped open the phone to identify the caller.

Nicolette watched the frown deepen on his face as he snapped the phone shut and drop it back into his pocket.

"Not an emergency?"

"She probably thinks it is," he answered. "That was my mother."

"Oh. Well don't let me intrude. If you need to talk to her it won't bother me."

He sighed. "Thanks, but it isn't necessary. I already know what the call is about. A big fund-raiser is being held back in Houston this coming weekend for a congressman in my parents' district. She wants me to attend and refuses to accept that I won't be there."

She studied him thoughtfully. "You don't like politics?"

He released a humorless laugh. "Politics has nothing to do with it. I don't want to spend my free time at big social galas of any sort. I have more important things to do."

Nicolette was digesting his comment when the waitress arrived with tortilla chips, hot salsa and tall drinks of iced tea. After the young woman had served them, Nicolette plucked a chip from the basket and dipped it into the salsa.

"Do you have siblings?" she asked him.

He shook his head. "I wish. It's hell being an only child."

Nicolette munched the chip, then said, "I wouldn't know what being an only child would feel like. I have a younger brother and sister. So my mother spreads her attention among all of us."

"Lucky you," he muttered and his features tightened as he reached for his tea. "Don't get me wrong, Nicolette. My mother is a loving person in her own way. But she can be smothering. It was really hard on her when I left for college and medical school. She, uh, you see, my father is always working. Always. So I guess she used me to fill the vacant spot."

Nicolette was beginning to get the picture and it wasn't a pretty one. "What do your parents think about you moving to this area?"

A sardonic expression twisted his features. "My father refuses to say more than hello to me. And my mother still believes I'll change my mind and return to Houston. One of these days she's going to realize that will never happen."

"You sound sure of that."

His brown eyes hardened with conviction.

"Never been more sure of anything, Nicolette. When you grow up watching your
parents do everything wrong, you grow up
determined to be different."

She could feel the undercurrent of tension
in his voice and it told her the issues he had
with his family were not small matters. The
urge to ask him more questions surged up in
her, but she bit them back. It wouldn't do to
let him think she was *that* interested. She
didn't want to give him any reason to think
she was looking at him as a man rather than
a doctor and colleague.

Thankfully, the waitress arrived with their
meal, and they spent the next few minutes
digging into their food and exchanging small
talk about the clinic.

In spite of it being eons since she'd sat
across the table from a man other than her
brother or cousins, Nicolette began to relax.
It was nice to be out, to be talking, to have a
man looking at her as though she were lovely
and interesting.

"Tell me, Nicolette—"

"Nicci," she interrupted. "Everyone calls
me Nicci, so you might as well, too. My
name got cut short as a child and it stuck."

He grinned and his eyes twinkled teasingly

as they roamed her face. "Little Nicci. Sounds tomboyish. Were you?"

Her cheeks warm, she chuckled softly. "Terribly. I cried when Mother made me wear a dress to church."

"Well, you obviously grew out of it," he said as he recalled her long, beautiful legs exposed beneath the hem of her skirt and the sexy high heels on her feet. She was the essence of femininity and every inch of her pulled on him like a mighty magnet.

"I grew out of a lot of things," she replied with a sigh.

Ridge shoveled up the last bite of enchilada and while he ate it, he studied her expression, which had suddenly become sober. Even though she smiled and laughed and joked at times, he could feel sadness emanating from her, as though her spirit had been broken. He hated that notion and realized he'd like to heal her heart.

"What made you decide to become a physician's assistant, Nicci?"

She pushed the last few bites of food around on her plate. "I always wanted to help people, and in high school I decided I wanted to become a nurse and work as a missionary. But while I was in nursing school, I realized

I could be of more help if I could actually doctor the needy. So I went a step further with my education."

Ridge studied her downcast face and the way her brown hair waved against her cheek. She had a thick, glorious head of hair. The color was as rich as ground coffee beans and glistened like moonlight on water. Several times he'd caught himself wanting to reach out and touch the strands, to see for himself if they were really as silky as they looked.

"What happened with the missionary work? I mean, you're obviously living and working here," he said.

The corners of her mouth turned downward. "I met Bill in college, and after we married my plans…got changed. I have done some relief work in Mexico and the Philippines, though. And maybe someday I'll go back to do more."

Her gaze lifted and as her eyes met his he felt a physical jolt. The sensation stirred him and had him wondering what it would be like to have her touching him intimately, to have her soft drawl whispering in his ear.

She asked, "Have you ever done any relief work?"

Clearing his throat, he said, "Only here in

the States." Then he added mockingly, "My parents think I'm doing relief work now."

She frowned with confusion. "Excuse me?"

He wished he could laugh. He wished he could forget the sight of his parents staring down their noses at him, trying their best to make him feel guilty and ungrateful. It hadn't worked. He wouldn't let it work.

"The fact that I'm practicing here in a small city," he explained. "Instead of in Houston where the money and prestige are. They think I'm making peanuts and wasting my education."

Still frowning, she said, "Money and prestige have nothing to do with healing people."

He gave a half grin. "I'm glad someone around here besides me understands that." He threw down his napkin and reached for the ticket the waitress had left on the outer corner of the table. "If you're finished, we'd better go. I have a one-o'clock appointment."

Nodding, Nicolette reached for her handbag. "I need to be getting back, too."

Ridge paid the bill and the two of them left the restaurant. As he drove them the short distance to the clinic, he asked, "Your brother and sister, what do they do?"

"Lex helps our cousins, Matt and Cordero, run the ranch. He mainly manages sales and shipping. Matt is general manager and Cordero is in charge of the horses. Of course, most of the time all three of them labor with the rest of the wranglers. As for my sister, Mercedes, she's presently in the Air Force and serving at Camp Justice over in Diego Garcia."

"Must be nice to be a part of a big family," he mused out loud. "I'd like to meet them someday."

Nicolette could just imagine the buzz she'd create if she invited Ridge out to the ranch. She'd fiercely resisted her family's nagging to find herself a boyfriend. If Ridge showed up for supper they'd think she'd either gone totally crazy or that she'd soon be sporting an engagement ring.

She glanced over at his rugged profile, then allowed her gaze to drift downward over his lean torso and long legs. The sight of him reminded her of all that she'd been missing and everything she'd been trying to forget. Yet the hollow feeling in her chest wasn't enough to make her look away or to keep her from saying, "Maybe you'd like to come out to the ranch for supper sometime?"

By now they were at the clinic. He pulled

into the nearest parking slot and turned off the engine before he turned in the seat to look at her.

"Are you serious?"

No, she was crazy, Nicolette thought. This man was nine years younger than her. Anything between them would be wrong and never work. But she'd offered the invitation and she wasn't about to go back on it now.

"Yes, I'm asking you out to the ranch for supper. You said you'd like to see it and meet my family. Here's your chance," she said with a cheery casualness she was far from feeling.

He let out a long breath, and then a wide smile spread across his face. "You've surprised me, Nicci. I'm almost wondering if this is some sort of trick."

"Trick? Why would I do something like that to you?"

A deep, rough chuckle rumbled up from his chest. "Nicci, Nicci," he said with wry censure, taking hold of her hand, "you know you dislike me for taking Dr. Walters's place."

Nicolette turned her head away from him as streaks of sizzling heat jumped from his fingers into hers. "That's not right. I mean, I loved Dr. Walters and I hated to see him go. But it's not your fault that the man retired."

"Hmmm. Well, I got the impression last night that you—" his voice lowered to a purr "—didn't want anything to do with me personally."

Her expression wary, she looked back at him. "Is that what this is, personal?"

His hand slid up her arm until his warm fingers were curved around the side of her neck. Nicolette's insides began to burn and melt, and she wondered why she didn't have the strength to get out of the truck and away from him.

"It is for me," he murmured. "From the moment I first laid eyes on you, it became personal."

She tried to suck in a deep breath, but all her lungs could manage was a shallow sip of air.

"Ridge, I'm nine years older than you."

His face dipped closer to hers. "Who's counting?"

She nervously licked her lips. "I am. And besides that, I'm not interested in…romance. Not with you or any man."

"Well, I'm just going to have to do my best to change your mind," he whispered.

Nicolette saw his kiss coming, but she

didn't have the strength to turn her head or pull away. Instead, just as his mouth was about to settle over hers, her eyelids fluttered down, her lips parted.

The contact was just long enough to allow her to taste him, to feel the hard contours of his lips molding against hers. Then it was over and she was staring at him in lost wonder.

"When do I show up for supper?" he asked. "Saturday?"

From the corner of her eye, Nicolette caught a flash of movement in front of the truck. Instantly she jerked away from him to see a group of nurses walking across the parking lot. At least two of the women were glancing their way, and she could only guess at what they were thinking.

"Now look what you've done!" she exclaimed. "Those nurses probably saw us kissing. By this evening, gossip about the two of us will be all over the clinic!"

"Good," he said with a grin. "I want everyone to know that you're going to be my woman."

His woman! What was he, some sort of modern-day caveman? No, she would never belong to any man again, Nicolette silently vowed. And the sooner she got that message across to Dr. Ridge Garroway, the better off they'd both be.

Skewering his chest with her forefinger, she said in a gritty voice, "Look, Doctor, get this through your head now. I will never, *ever* be your, or any man's, woman! Your friend, maybe. But never your woman!"

Unaffected by her harsh outburst, Ridge gently patted her face and gave her a wicked smile. "We'll see, Nicci. We'll see."

Chapter Four

Later that evening, Ridge pulled to a stop in front of his house to see Corey, his new teenage handyman, waiting for him on the front verandah. Enoch, Ridge's German shepherd, was snuggled up to the teenager's side, panting with a silly grin at the fact that he had company.

"Hi, Mr. Ridge!" The tall, slim boy with bright-red hair jumped from the porch and jogged out to meet his employer. "You got home early this evening. Not as many sick people today?"

Ridge climbed from the truck and pulled

a briefcase after him. "There were plenty of sick people, Corey. I just happened to take care of them a bit more quickly today. Been waiting long?"

Corey was fourteen years old and lived with his mother in a small house a mile or so down the rural road from Ridge. He'd met the boy at a local church gathering that had been given just so Ridge would have the opportunity to meet his new neighbors. At that time he'd learned Corey's mother worked at a local grocery store as a checker. It wasn't until later, after he'd hired Corey to help him with chores around the place, that the boy had told Ridge he didn't have a father. Apparently, the man had left the family when Corey was only a few months old.

Corey shook his head. "No. Just a few minutes. I came early so I could check on Enoch's water bowl. I wouldn't want him to go thirsty. With it being so hot and all."

"No. We certainly wouldn't want that," Ridge agreed as he strode toward the house. Corey followed closely at his heels with the dog bounding happily in front of them. Enoch's water bowl was a galvanized foot tub that held enough water for five dogs to drink for several days. It was obvious the boy loved the German shepherd and used any excuse to spend as much time with the dog as he could. Ridge was grateful that his pet had companionship while he was away at work.

"Oh, yeah, I ate a sandwich before I walked over. I'm fine."

"Well, why don't you come in the house and drink a soda while I change clothes. And then we'll get to work on that fence."

Ridge reached to open the wooden screen door, but Corey hung back. Ridge glanced around to see a sheepish expression on the boy's freckled face. "What's wrong? If you don't want a soda, that's fine. Just tell me."

The teenager's face turned ruddy. "It ain't that, Mr. Ridge. My mom says I'm not to go into your house. She says that would be—intruding."

Obviously the boy's mother was trying to teach him manners, and Ridge respected her effort. Especially when Lillian, his own mother, had been just the opposite and had pushed Ridge to insert himself into any situation where he might benefit.

Slapping the boy's shoulder with affection, he said, "Only if I didn't invite you,

Corey. Now come on. I'll personally tell your mother that it's okay with me."

"You will?"

"Sure."

"What about Enoch? Can he come in, too?"

Since the dog already had his nose stuck in the crack between the wooden screen door and the casing, it was clear he didn't want to be left out.

"Yeah," Ridge said with an indulgent grin, "he can come, too."

Ridge opened the door, and the dog shot into the house. Corey followed and Ridge led the way to the kitchen. After he'd given the boy a soda and Enoch a bowl of treats, he hurried to the bedroom to change into jeans, T-shirt and boots.

A few minutes later, man, boy and dog left the house and walked through the hazy heat of late afternoon until they reached a spot in the pasture where Ridge was replacing sagging barbed wire and rotted cedar posts.

The ground on Ridge's land consisted of soil that locals referred to as black gumbo. It was rich, black clay and would grow anything planted in it. However, there were drawbacks. When wet, the clay weighed a ton and stuck to everything, and when dry, it was as hard as cement. Unfortunately, weather the past few weeks had been dry and digging with a hand-held posthole digger was arduous and slow going.

"Let me do it, Mr. Ridge. You're getting hot and tired," Corey insisted.

Ridge stepped back from the digger and allowed Corey to take control of the two wooden handles. He doubted the boy could hack out more than an inch or two but he understood the teenager wanted to earn his pay.

"What we need, Corey," Ridge said as he wiped his sweaty face with a handkerchief, "is a tractor and an augur. But I haven't had time to buy one. Maybe soon I'll come up with one."

Corey paused from his digging long enough to look at Ridge. "Oh, don't do that, Mr. Ridge. Then you wouldn't need me."

Ridge laughed. "Don't worry, Corey. Even with a tractor I'll have plenty of work for you. There're horses to feed and Enoch has to be taken care of. And there's repair work to be done on the barn and the chicken house."

The boy's face split into an eager grin. "Boy, that sounds like years of work! I'll be around for a long time," he said, then screwed his nose up with a new thought.

"Why are you gonna fix that old chicken house? You don't want chickens, do you?"

"Sure. Why not? You like eggs, don't you?"

Still frowning, Corey said, "Yeah. But you can buy eggs at the store."

"Most everything can be bought at stores, Corey, it's not that. A man likes to do for himself sometimes. Makes having things more special. You know what I mean?"

Corey tilted his head toward one thin shoulder as he contemplated Ridge's words. "Guess so. Sorta like when I made my mom a flowerpot out of a coffee can. She said she liked it better than any of them from the store cause I'd made it."

Pleased that the boy understood, Ridge nodded. "That's exactly what I mean, Corey."

"Boy, I know one thing, if you do all those things around here, you're gonna have some kind of mansion," Corey remarked as he turned his attention back to the digging.

The place was going to be far from a mansion, Ridge thought, and that was just the way he wanted it.

Back in Houston, the Garroway home had been a huge showplace of carefully deco-rated rooms used to entertain and impress the people in his parent's social circle. Ridge had never felt warm or sheltered there. Not when his father had been mostly gone and his mother prone to histrionic episodes of yelling and weeping.

By the time Ridge had reached the age of ten, he'd silently vowed that when he grew up, his life, his home, his friends would be different. So far he'd kept that vow. But now as he looked around this place that was becoming his home, he was seeing a woman in it. And he couldn't begin to imagine what she would think about a small, three-bedroom house with an old-fashioned verandah on two sides.

Nicci. He was still finding it difficult to believe that she'd gone to lunch with him. But it was the kiss, the sweet, brief meeting of their lips that was playing over and over in his mind. Ridge had experienced some mind-bending kisses before, but this thing with Nicci had been different in so many ways. The fleeting contact had opened his eyes and when he'd looked at her, he'd seen more than a beautiful, desirable woman he wanted to make love to. He'd seen a woman he wanted to draw to his side, to protect and cherish.

None of his feelings made sense. Especially when Nicci was from a rich family and more than likely wouldn't be content to step down from that type of lifestyle, an existence he was doing his best to get away from. Besides that, she'd already insisted that she didn't want a man in her life. How many more obstacles did he need to convince him that the woman was all wrong for him, he wondered wryly.

"No, it's not going to be anything close to a mansion, Corey. Just a little ranch that I can call home. That's all I want."

Corey pounded the blades at the hard earth. "Well, all I can say is that you must be mighty smart, Mr. Ridge, to be a doctor. Mom says it takes a lot of smarts to go to medical school."

Ridge chuckled. "It's not easy, but if a person wants to do something bad enough he'll work hard and get through." He watched the boy struggle to make a dent in the hole they were digging, and restrained himself from taking over. "What about your schooling, Corey? Do you make good grades?"

"Oh, they're pretty good." Grimacing, he swiped at the sweat slipping into his eyes. "'Cept for algebra. I'm taking a summer class to do that over."

"Maybe you need a little extra help," Ridge suggested. "Does your mother help you with homework?"

"Yeah. She helps me with everything but Algebra. She wasn't too good at that subject, either, and she says she can't remember how to do it."

"Sounds like you need a tutor," Ridge said, while wondering whom he might hire to help the boy.

Out of breath from his exertion with the digger, Corey stopped and looked at him. "That's what Mom says. But I don't know anybody who'd help." His eyes suddenly widened with a new thought. "Mr. Ridge, if I brought my math book in the evenings on some days, do you think—I mean could you help me a little? I'd be willing for you to keep my wages on those days. I wouldn't want you to do it for nothin'."

I don't have time. Ridge was thinking the words, but he didn't say them. And he wouldn't say them. Not when he'd heard them over and over from his own father and each time the neglect and indifference of those words had struck him like stones. This boy didn't deserve that sort of treatment any more than Ridge had. Somehow, he would find time to help Corey.

"I'd be glad to, Corey. But you'll still get your wages like promised. We'll do the studying after work, okay?"

Corey smiled and attacked the posthole with renewed vigor. "Boy, Mr. Ridge, I sure am glad you moved here."

Later that evening at the Sandbur, Nicolette was walking through the great room in search of her mother when Lex bellowed down from the staircase landing.

"Mother! Where is my leather duffel bag? Who's taken it from my room?"

Geraldine stepped into the room, obviously searching for the source of the yelling. Immediately she spotted Nicolette and with a smile rolled her eyes upward toward Lex.

"It's in the kitchen, Lex. Alida took it there to clean it," she patiently called up to her son, then walked over to where Nicolette stood near the end of a sofa. "I didn't realize you were home, sweetheart. Ready for supper?"

Nicolette kissed her mother's cheek. "As soon as I change clothes. Where's Lex going?"

"To Florida. There's a buyer there that thinks he wants to purchase some of our Brahmans. Lex wants to convince him in person," she added with a cheeky smile. "Once he gets there I hope he keeps the yelling down."

Nicolette chuckled. "My brother not yelling? You've got to be kidding."

"I heard that, you little minx," Lex teased as he bounded down the staircase to join his mother and sister. He kissed Nicolette's cheek, then turned a pointed look on his mother. "I talked to Ramsey this morning. He wants to take me deep sea fishing, so I'll probably be gone through the weekend."

Nicolette rolled her eyes at him. "Deep sea fishing! I thought this was a cattle sale deal." Giving her mother a conspiring wink, she said, "I think Matt needs to hear about this. While he's working his butt off, Lex is going fishing. Don't think this is going to go over well with our cousin."

Lex gave his sister a good-natured frown. "Now look, sissy, a buyer has to be made happy. Makes his wallet open wider, you know. And if fishing is his thing, I've got to go along."

Smiling with indulgence, she said, "Yeah, yeah. Excuses, excuses. Tell them to your cousins." Her expression sobering, she glanced from her brother to her mother, then back again. "Actually, I hope you have a good time. But I'm sorry you're going to be gone. I'm…inviting someone out to the ranch this weekend. I wanted you to meet him."

As soon as Nicolette's words were out, Lex and Geraldine were staring at her as though she was feverish.

"Him?" Geraldine questioned.

"A man!" Lex exclaimed with surprise.

Nicolette folded her arms against her breasts in an unconsciously protective gesture. "It's not like it sounds. He's…a colleague. The doctor who has taken Dr. Walters's place."

"He's still a man, isn't he?" Lex pointed out with a wicked waggle of his brows.

Ignoring her son's suggestive teasing, Geraldine said to Nicolette, "How nice, dear. But I thought—" She broke off with a puzzled frown. "The other night you said he was too young and brash, and you gave me the impression you didn't like him."

Nicolette breathed deeply. *Like* was simply too meek a word for how she felt about Ridge. The man stirred up all sorts of feelings in her. And after that lunchtime kiss—well, she hadn't been able to focus on anything but him during the remainder of the afternoon.

Drat him. He'd had no business catching her off guard like that.

But you'd seen the little kiss coming, Nicci, and you did nothing to stop it.

Pushing aside that pestering voice in her head, she said to her mother, "Well, since he treated Dan I've changed my mind. He seems to really care about people and I'm willing to be…friends with the man."

"Friends!" Lex said with a groan of disgust. "You need more than a friend, sissy. How old did you say this guy is? Maybe I'd better call off my trip to Florida so I can scope him out."

Nicolette pursed her lips. "He's twenty-nine. And no, you definitely need to go to Florida. I wouldn't have you miss the fishing for the world."

Chuckling, Lex patted her cheek. "I'll catch him next time."

There wouldn't be a next time, Nicolette wanted to say. The invitation she'd made to Ridge to come to the Sandbur, she'd blurted out on impulse. Next time she would be more careful to watch what she said and especially what she did around the man.

"Is the good doctor going to be eating dinner with us, Nicolette?"

Her mother's question brought Nicolette's attention away from Lex and back to Geraldine. "Yes, on Saturday evening. I thought I'd show him around the ranch before we ate. He's interested in raising a few cattle and horses. That's why I thought he might enjoy touring the ranch."

"Very nice of you, sweetheart. And I'm glad you got over your stiff-necked attitude toward the man. I know how lost you were when Dr. Walters left, so becoming friends with this man can only be good for you."

Nicolette wasn't so sure about that, but it was obvious her announcement about Ridge had made Geraldine and Lex happy. So if they wanted to think she'd gotten herself a new man, then let them. They'd find out soon enough where Ridge really stood in her life.

"Now," Geraldine went on, as she looped her arm through Nicolette's and urged her out of the great room. "If you don't have anything particular in mind for the dinner Saturday night, I think I'll send Alida down to Seadrift to buy some fresh seafood. Maybe some flounder and drum, and of course, several pounds of shrimp. The shrimp boats should be going out daily now. What do you think?"

Nicolette stifled a sigh. "I think you're

going to too much trouble, Mother. A steak will be fine."

"Steak! Not on your life!" she exclaimed, then, wrinkling her forehead in contemplation, she added, "Unless I add it to the seafood. But I'll let Cook make that decision." She leaned over and kissed Nicolette's cheek. "Now you go change your clothes for supper. I'm going to call Matt and Juliet and tell them not to make plans for Saturday night."

So much for keeping the evening mundane, Nicolette thought helplessly. By the time Ridge arrived on the ranch, her family would probably have welcoming banners up to greet him.

Saturday morning, Nicolette rose early and after having breakfast with her mother, quickly dressed in jeans, boots and a sleeveless, butter-colored blouse that laced up the front. While she French-braided her long brown hair and patted on a dab of face powder and pale-pink lipstick, she decided she would call Ridge and invite him to come out to the ranch this morning.

It wasn't that she was *that* eager to see the man, she told herself. After all, she worked in the same building with him. If she'd wanted to see him, she could simply have walked down the hallway to his office. And moving her invitation up to this morning had nothing to do with the fact that she hadn't heard from the man since she'd left him in the parking lot where he'd planted that unexpected kiss on her.

A part of Nicolette had expected him to at least call her office and confirm their supper date. But she'd neither seen nor heard from the man during the last four days and she'd begun to wonder about his intentions toward her.

What intentions? she sarcastically asked herself. The man was a playboy. The only intentions he had were to have fun. Only, she had news for him. She wasn't going to be his latest amusement.

Five minutes later she picked up the telephone in her bedroom and dialed Ridge's cell phone number. He answered after the second ring, and the moment she heard his deep voice her heart became a traitor to her plan to be unaffected by the man.

"Ridge, this is Nicci," she quickly replied. "I was calling to see if you were still planning to come out to the ranch for supper."

"Nicci!" he said her name with a measure of surprise. "I wasn't expecting to hear from you so early this morning."

She glanced at the small watch strapped to her wrist. It was only eight-thirty, but with her busy hours that was like the middle of the morning. "Uh, I didn't wake you, did I?"

He laughed. "Sorry to spoil your image of me, Nicci, but I don't laze around in bed. I was about to call my hired help to see how soon he could be here. I've got a stack of cedar posts to put in."

Not trusting herself with the image of a nude Ridge lounging in bed, Nicolette pushed her thoughts forward. "Oh. Then your day is already tied up?" she asked.

"Not yet. Why?"

She drew in a bracing breath. "Nothing important," she said with as much casualness as her hammering heart would allow. "I was going to see if you'd like to come out to the ranch this morning. I'll have the wranglers saddle a couple of mounts for us and we can ride over some of the ranch. I thought riding horseback would be a nice way for you to view the property."

There was a long pause and Nicolette figured she'd taken him by surprise. But not nearly as much as she'd surprised herself, she thought dryly. Asking to spend any more time than necessary with the flirtatious doctor was riskier than dancing around a flaming fire while carrying a gallon of gas on her back.

"Nicci, you've bowled me over," he finally answered. "When the caller ID flashed up your name I figured you were calling to cancel our supper completely. Actually, all week I've been expecting you to call and do just that."

Pleased to hear that he wasn't taking her for granted, she smiled. "Do you want me to cancel my invitation?"

"Are you kidding?" he quickly retorted, then added, "I'll be there as soon as I can change clothes."

He ended their connection before Nicolette could give him directions. She punched Redial and he answered before the first ring finished.

"What's wrong?" he asked.

"Don't you need directions on how to get here?"

He chuckled. "Sorry, Nicci. I'm a little excited."

About seeing her or the ranch, she wanted to ask. But she wasn't about to goad him with such a loaded question. Especially when she'd promised herself that she was only going to be Ridge's friend and nothing else.

Still, she had to quell her own excitement as she assured him that she'd be watching for his arrival.

A little more than thirty minutes later, Nicolette was sitting in one of the wicker chairs on the front porch when Ridge's red truck drove up the short driveway that circled in front of the Sandbur's main house.

The morning was already hot and the sun fierce. She pulled a battered straw cowboy hat down on her forehead as she walked out to greet him.

"I see you made it without any problem."

Turning away from the truck, he gave her the same devilish smile he'd given her the first day he'd walked into her waiting room at the clinic. This morning he was dressed as any cowboy here on the ranch would be dressed for a day of work, in a pair jeans and boots and a cool cotton shirt. A brown cowboy hat shaded his face. It suited his lean features. In fact, his rugged appearance was far too appealing for Nicolette's own good, and she told herself not to stare or let her imagination be carried away by his striking image.

"No problems at all," he replied. "Once I

turned off the main highway I remembered you saying to ignore all the little side roads. There certainly were plenty of those."

"I'm glad you could make it this morning," she said, extending her hand to him.

He wrapped his hand around hers, but rather than giving it a shake of greeting, he bent his head and placed a quick kiss on her cheek. "I'm glad, too," he murmured. "Thank you for asking me."

Well, so much for starting out on friendly terms, Nicolette thought, as she glanced back toward the house. Had her mother seen that? Dear Lord, she hoped not. The woman was already making too much of Ridge's visit. A little kiss, even a peck on the cheek, was enough to get the cogs whirling in her match-making head.

"I'm sorry for interrupting your fence building," she told him. "I understand how limited your free time is."

He smiled. In the few days they'd been apart, she'd forgotten just how potent his presence was. Now that she'd been reminded, Nicolette decided the day was going to be one long temptation, one that she would have to fight with all her might.

"Don't worry about it. The fence will get

built. Besides, I'd much rather spend time with you than pound out a row of postholes."

Dimples appeared on both sides of his mouth as he spoke the last words. Nicolette did her best to ignore them as she pulled on his hand and urged him toward the house.

"Before we walk down to the barn, let's go in and I'll introduce you to Mother," she told him. "Cook has a thermos and a light lunch packed for our saddlebags. So we need to pick up those things from the kitchen."

As the two of them walked to the house, Ridge looked around him with appreciation. "This is beautiful, Nicci. The house is nice without being ostentatious. Everything looks like people actually live here. I even see some brown spots on the lawn, and there are two dogs on the front porch."

Surprised by his comment, she laughed. "People do live here and we like to be comfortable. In fact, at one time, two families lived in this one house. Along with my brother and my parents, there were also my aunt and uncle, plus my cousins Matt and Lucita. That was before my sister, Mercedes, and my cousin Cordero were born."

"Sounds like a lot of togetherness," he said as they walked across the porch to the double wooden doors that served as the main entrance of the house.

Nicolette smiled with fond remembrance. "It was nice," she said. "Sometimes I miss the closeness of those days."

Ridge followed her into a small foyer. A hall tree held several old cowboy hats with bent brims and sweat-stained crowns. Along one wall sat an antique deacon's bench and an equally old buggy wheel made of wooden spokes. The remaining space was filled with a large assortment of huge, potted succulents, one of which was a prickly pear covered with bright yellow blooms.

"Where do your cousins live now?" he asked curiously. "Here on the ranch?"

She nodded. "There's another house just down the road from here. When we start out on the horses I'll show you."

Nicolette led him into a large living area and had just dropped her hold on his hand when a silver-haired woman appeared from a door on the left side of the room.

She was a tall, thin woman with a handsome face and an erect carriage that told him she was still very active. Like her daughter, she was dressed in jeans, and her long hair was pulled into a clasp at her nape.

"Mother," Nicolette called to her. "Come and meet Dr. Garroway."

Smiling warmly, the woman approached him with an extended hand. "Hello, Dr. Garroway. I'm Geraldine Saddler, Nicci's mother. Welcome to the Sandbur."

Ridge shook her hand. She was the total opposite of his own mother. One glance at Geraldine's face was all it took for him to see she was a woman of strong character. He very much doubted she'd ever shirked from any unpleasant task she'd been faced with down through the years.

"It's a pleasure to be here. And Nicci didn't have to tell me that you were a lovely woman. I had already suspected you would be, and now I can see for myself that I was right."

Geraldine laughed with pleasure. "Dr. Garroway, in this house flattery will get you everything."

Smiling, he released her hand. "Call me Ridge," he invited. "I leave the doctor part at the clinic."

Her green eyes sparkled as she glanced from him to her daughter and back to him again. "Only if you'll call me Geraldine," she insisted, then motioned for the two of them to follow her. "Let's go to the kitchen and I'll help Cook gather up your lunches. Ridge, would you like something to drink before the two of you leave on your ride? Coffee, a soda or beer?"

"Thank you, but I'm fine. I drank a cup of coffee on my drive out here."

The three of them left the great room and entered a long hallway. Every few feet there were doors leading off to the left and the right. With some of the entrances open, Ridge could see glimpses of the rooms beyond. Surprisingly everything looked comfortable, homey and used. Unlike the many rooms in his parents home where, as a child, he'd been forbidden to enter.

By the time he'd grown into his teenage years, he'd narrowed his living space down to two rooms in the massive house. The kitchen and his bedroom had been the only places he'd felt comfortable. In his bedroom he'd been able to shut himself away from the constant bickering between his parents and the phony adoration they had displayed with each other when guests were visiting. Whenever Ridge had felt the need to talk to someone other than his peers, he'd sat in the kitchen with the cook and her helper, two women who'd displayed three times more common sense than his mother ever had.

As for his father, Richard Garroway had rarely had time for his son and whenever he'd made time, he'd used it to preach to Ridge about the importance of a man making a success of himself. According to his father, a man's wealth was determined by the sum of his bank account.

"Ridge? Is anything wrong?" Nicolette's hand lightly touched his. He pulled himself out of his thoughts to glance over at her. She was studying him with a look of concern.

"No," he answered. "Why do you ask?"

She paused in the hallway, leaving Geraldine to go on ahead of them. "The look on your face," she said to him. "Are you…feeling uncomfortable here in my home?"

Uncomfortable? Not here, not with her, not ever, Ridge realized.

Smiling with an ease he'd never felt before, he curled his arm around her shoulders and urged her forward. "Believe me, Nicci, I've never felt more at home."

Chapter Five

Moments later the three of them reached the end of the hallway, and Geraldine pushed her way through two louvered swinging doors. Ridge followed behind Nicci as they entered a kitchen equipped with old, industrial-size appliances and a long pine worktable flanked by wooden benches.

A tall, bony woman who looked to be in her seventies was occupied at a large wooden cutting board. She was busily plucking fresh shrimp from a huge mound and pinching the heads off. As he and the two women trouped into the room, she looked up from her work and wiped her hands on the tail of her apron.

"Cook, this is Dr. Ridge Garroway," Geraldine said. "Ridge, this is our devoted Hattie—but everyone calls her Cook. She's been with us for over forty years, so she's family."

Cook's red lips pursed with sarcastic humor at Geraldine. "Why did you have to tell him how long I've been around here? Now he'll know how old I am!"

She extended her hand to Ridge and he noticed her fingernails were painted the same color as her lips. Her black hair had only threads of gray, and in spite of her advanced years, she was a comely woman.

"Nice to meet you, Cook. I hope my being here for supper hasn't caused you a lot of extra work."

The older woman let out a mocking laugh as she eyed Ridge with open appreciation. "Geraldine has made a menu longer than my arm. I'll be working my rear off all day."

"Cook!" Nicolette scolded with embarrassment.

Ignoring Nicolette's dismay, Cook continued to chuckle. "Well, it's a big deal for Nicci to be bringing a man to the ranch. We haven't seen her with one in years, you know, so we've planned a feast."

With one raised brow, he turned a speculative grin on Nicolette. "No man at all. Really?" he asked.

"There's no need for you to answer that question, Cook," Nicci firmly inserted.

Casting an impish look at Ridge, Cook said, "Well, I'd better not go into that. I don't want to get my doctor mad at me." Her black eyes swept up and down the length of him. "I haven't seen a man as good-looking as you since Neil Rankin swept in here from New Mexico and married our little Raine. What kind of doctoring do you do, Ridge?"

Enjoying her thoroughly, Ridge raised her hand to his lips and kissed the back of it. "I'm a heart doctor, Miss Hattie. You don't have any heart problems, do you?"

Cook laughed and blushed as he finally dropped her hand. "The only heart problem I have is a lack of a love life. Can you do anything about that, doc?"

Ridge laughed with her. "I'm not sure. I guess I could introduce you to some of my single patients."

Exchanging a conspiratorial wink with

Ridge, Nicci said to the woman, "Ridge is the doctor who got Dan back on his feet, Cook. So you might want to thank him for that."

With a quick snort, Cook waved a dismissive hand at both Ridge and Nicci. "That old codger! He's not romance material. I just sent him that box of cookies because I felt sorry for him."

"I thought it was because you were a little sweet on the old wrangler," Nicci suggested.

With a loud groan of protest, Cook turned and headed back to the cutting board. "Keep that up, girl, and you won't get any lunch, much less supper," she warned.

The bantering between the women kept up for ten more minutes while Cook finished putting their lunches together.

When Ridge and Nicolette finally exited the kitchen through a back door, he was carrying a pair of stuffed saddlebags and two canteens of cold water. From the edge of the patio, Cook and Geraldine were smiling broadly and waving them off as if they were headed out on a great expedition.

As the two of them walked in the direction of the barn, Ridge said, "I think your mother and Cook liked me."

Nicolette laughed. "I'm sorry to bust your

bubble, Ridge, but I think they would like any male I brought home."

"Oh," he said with wry amusement. "And I thought it was my dazzling personality."

She glanced over at him and smiled. She'd not expected him to be so friendly and down-to-earth with her family, especially with Cook. Bill had believed he was above mixing and mingling with the hired help, which had always irked Nicolette, who considered Cook and the other hands on the Sandbur family. Her ex-husband's superior attitude had made their visits home very awkward, until she'd finally started leaving Bill to his own pursuits and making the trips down from San Antonio by herself. No doubt he'd used those times alone to entertain his women, she thought bitterly. But that was in the past, and she needed to heed her mother's advice and forget the hurt and betrayal.

"I'm only kidding, Ridge. Mother and Cook do like you. But you'll have to wait until tonight to see if my cousins cotton to you," she teased.

"What about your brother, won't he be here?"

She shook her head. "Lex had to go to Florida to see a potential cattle buyer."

"Oh. That's too bad," Ridge replied. "If he's anything like your mother, I know I'd like him."

It was on the tip of Nicolette's tongue to tell Ridge he could meet Lex the next time he visited. But then she'd sworn to herself that this one invitation was all she was going to give him. Yet as she walked along with him, she realized that idea was a dour one. She was enjoying having him here, enjoying being at his side and seeing the lighthearted smiles on his face. He made her feel young and alive. Did she really never want to experience this again?

"Uh, speaking of your family," his voice broke into her thoughts, "I'm curious about Cook. Does she not have any relatives of her own?"

"She has a sister and a niece and nephew that live up near Cuero, but she doesn't have any children of her own. Her husband, Herbert, was killed in the Vietnam War in 1965. He was a lieutenant in the Marine Corp so he was pretty much in the thick of battle. Cook had already been working here on the Sandbur for several years when it happened, and Mother said the whole ranch was devastated by the news. She and Herbert had been young and very much in love when he went to war. Afterwards, well, she never married again."

"Hmm," Ridge mused aloud. "I wonder why? She was obviously a very beautiful woman in her day."

Warm color filled Nicolette's cheeks. She couldn't remember the last time she'd discussed such romantic things with a man, and it left her feeling a little embarrassed. Especially when she kept trying to think of Ridge as a friend instead of a suitor.

"Cook says a woman only has one real love in her life—anything after that is just for laughs."

"Is that the way you think, Nicci?"

Nicolette didn't know whether it was his question or a rock on the path that caused her to stumble. Either way, the moment the toe of her boot tripped, Ridge's strong hand caught her elbow and steadied her.

As they paused on the beaten trail, Nicolette looked up at his warm brown eyes, until the breathless feeling in her chest became too much for her. She looked away, toward the barn where their horses were waiting.

"I, uh, don't think about those things anymore, Ridge," she answered, then quickly strode ahead of him.

By the time he caught up to her they were only a short distance from the barn, and Ridge decided the moment for him to press her about her opinions on love had passed. Which was probably for the best. The morning had been far more pleasant than he'd ever expected and he didn't want to ruin the rest of the day.

"Are those the horses we'll be riding?" he asked, pointing to the pair of saddled mounts tethered to a scraggily mesquite tree.

"No. Ours are over there."

She pointed to a holding pen that was attached to the east end of a huge barn made of corrugated steel. In one corner of the pen, two horses, a sorrel and a gray, were tethered to a wooden hitching post.

Pickup trucks, most of them sporting scratches and dents from heavy ranch use, were parked here and there among the outbuildings and cattle pens. Cowboys were milling about, some spreading feed in long troughs for a herd of gray Brahmans, while others were loading molasses licks on the back of a flatbed truck.

Before they made their way over to the horses, Nicolette introduced him to several of the busy wranglers, then pointed out a few of the nearest outbuildings and ex-plained their use.

"What an operation," he exclaimed as he watched the busy comings and goings. "I can't imagine the job it takes to keep all this running smoothly. Obviously, the work doesn't stop even though it's the weekend."

She nodded. "Unfortunately the livestock don't care if it's Saturday or Sunday. But Matt tries to rotate all the men's hours so that they have equal time off. And Sunday mornings are always free for church. Even if some of the men are camped out on the ranch for roundup, one of the cowboys in the group will read scripture to the others."

His eyes were full of approval as he turned his gaze on hers. "Sounds like you all work as one big family."

The two of them were standing in the shade of the mesquite, but now Nicolette turned in the direction of the pen where their horses were waiting. "That's a tradition here on the Sandbur. I suppose that's why once a cowboy hires on, he's here for years."

"So you don't have trouble keeping good workers?"

"Oh, once in a while a bad apple comes along, but for the most part we have dedicated men. I suppose it's just the same as hospitals and clinics. There are some committed doctors and nurses and some just working to draw their money."

His brows arched warily as he glanced her way. "Hmm. I'm afraid to ask which bunch you put me in."

He watched a smile hesitate at the corners of her lips before it eventually spread across her face.

"Okay," she said, "I'll admit I had preconceived notions about you. But now—let's just say I'm willing to give you the benefit of the doubt."

He chuckled. "What kind of preconceived notion? Or should I not ask?"

By now they had reached a wide metal gate that opened into the holding pen. While Ridge unfastened the latch, Nicci stood to one side and waited for him to swing the gate open.

She said, "I'm sorry, but I thought you'd be one of those rich doctors in the business for the prestige and the money. And I guess I thought you were too young to be that serious about your job."

He followed her into the pen and carefully shut the gate behind them. "Being young isn't a crime," he told her. "And as for the money, I don't need it. If I never worked another day in my life, I have enough to comfortably survive. But then, my wants are simple, Nicci."

One delicate brow arched with skepticism, but she didn't make any comment. Instead, she gestured for him to follow her over to the tethered horses.

Rebel, the heavily muscled gray, was Ridge's horse for the day, and he carefully made friends with the animal before he tied on the saddlebags and slung a canteen over the horn.

In a few short minutes they were both mounted and riding west along a well-beaten trail through stands of mesquite trees and tall wesatch. Prickly pear was rampant and in some spots grew as tall as Rebel. Even so, grasses were abundant and they quickly came upon herds of gray Brahmans grazing on the more tender forage. For the most part the cattle were docile and content to simply raise their heads and watch the horses until they passed by.

Nicolette rode abreast of Ridge and he continually found his gaze drifting over to the beautiful picture she made. She sat a horse as though she'd been born there, which probably wasn't far from the truth. Her posture was straight without being stiff and because she rode a lengthy stirrup, her long legs were barely bent at the knee. More often than not, she had only one finger on the rein, which told Ridge she trusted her mount completely. He wondered what it would be like to have her absolute trust, to have her believe in him as a man, a doctor, a lover. No doubt her trust would empower a man and make him feel as though he could climb mountains.

"You ride really well, Ridge. When did you become familiar with horses?"

Ridge shook away his intimate thoughts as he answered her.

"I was probably about ten years old when I got on my first horse."

She looked surprised. "Your folks owned horses?"

His curt laugh was full of sarcasm. "No. My parents aren't outdoor people. My father's connection to the outdoors is to play a little golf and sit around the pool at the clubhouse. And my mother thinks the outdoors is strictly for insects and animals."

Beneath the brim of her hat, Nicci's brows pulled together in a thoughtful frown. "That's odd," she said, then glancing his way, she flicked a hand in his direction. "I mean, you ride a horse as well as any of our wranglers who've done it all their lives. You own cattle and horses, and yet you weren't brought up in this sort of lifestyle. You've made me curious now."

A wan smile lifted one corner of his mouth. "I have to thank Barry Macon for introducing me to ranching life. He was a childhood friend. We attended the same middle school together. That was before my parents took me out of public school," he added with a frown. "Anyway, Barry's parents owned a small ranch outside of Houston and that's where I first learned to ride. Barry's dad raised Black Angus and he would let us boys help him round up the cows for doctoring and vaccinating. And in the summertime we'd work in the hayfield driving tractors. I loved every minute of those days."

Enjoying the peek into his young life, she thoughtfully studied his face. "You spent a lot of time at Barry's home?" she asked.

"As much as I could. Their ranch was a little boy's paradise. Being around the animals, swimming in the creek, eating country meals at the Macons' kitchen table."

She heard more than just fond recollection in his voice. He was speaking with love. Something she'd not picked up on when he'd talked about his parents. It suddenly struck her that the Macon home had probably shaped his life in more ways than just fostering a love of ranching.

She said, "You say you met Barry while you were in public school. What happened to your friendship with Barry when you entered high school?"

Ridge's face tilted upward to the bright blue sky and the Mexican eagle gliding in lazy circles in the hot southern wind. He eyed the bird with respect and a bit of envy. Even though the black and white eagle had to forage alone for his survival, he was free to live as he wanted and not as someone else wished.

He answered Nicolette's question. "I didn't attend public high school. My parents sent me to boarding school. Which, in the long run, was actually better for me. I loved public school, but at boarding school I didn't have to live at home."

She stared at him with utter dismay. "My word, Ridge, was your home life really that bad?"

Sighing, he tugged the brim of his hat a little farther down on his forehead and fixed his gaze on the trail ahead of them. "I guess I've given you the wrong impression about my growing-up years, Nicci. You're probably thinking I'm giving you one of those poor-little-rich-kid stories."

As her gaze traveled over his strong profile, she tried to imagine him as a vulnerable child and her heart ached to think he'd grown up without the emotional support he'd needed from his parents.

"Are you?"

Shaking his head, he said, "No. I'll be the first to admit that I had things that kids like Barry never dreamed of having. We lived in a mansion, in the old, prominent part of the city. I had a closet full of well-tailored clothes, a new sports car every year, all the spending money I wanted, vacations to anyplace in the world, the best schools, medical care…you name it, I had it." A tight grimace came over his face as he glanced at her. "I guess I should have felt guilty as hell for not being satisfied. Indeed, my parents thought I needed therapy because I wasn't a happy kid. But I was happy—whenever I was away from them…when I was at Barry's and his mother was feeding us fried eggs and biscuits and gravy for breakfast. Can you understand any of that?"

Nodding, Nicolette said, "Yes, I can understand. You liked things simple—uncomplicated. So do I. That's why I moved back to the Sandbur after my divorce. This place keeps my feet on solid earth." Reaching up, she patted her horse's neck with a loving hand. "And where a person really feels at home is where he wants to be when he's wounded or lonely or in trouble."

He didn't say anything for long moments and as they rode along Nicolette contented herself with listening to the jingle of the bridle bits, the creak of the saddles, and the melodious twitter of the ever-present mockingbirds. She realized Ridge had probably already told her more about his personal life than he'd intended and, though she would have liked to know more, she wasn't going to push him.

After a few brief minutes passed in silence, he surprised her by picking up the conversation where she'd left off.

"I guess that's why I wanted to spend so much time at Barry's home. I never really felt at home with my parents. They've always been absorbed in themselves, and things weren't any different when I was a child. During the times the two of them were together there was always friction and fighting. To say the least, the atmosphere in the house was cold and strained. It's still that way."

Nicci knew that feeling quite well. The house she'd shared with Bill had eventually turned into a battleground. Now that she'd had a chance to look back on that awful time in her life, she was glad there had been no children to be hurt by the fallout, the way Ridge had apparently been hurt.

"Are your parents still together?"

He grunted mockingly. "Oh, yes. If you can call living under the same roof as being together. They go their separate ways—if you understand my meaning. In both of their opinions, divorce would be too expensive."

"I see," she murmured, and not for the first time, she realized how blessed her childhood had been. Her parents had been madly in love and they'd encompassed their children in that love. The rich sweetness of their relationship had permeated the house and made it a warm haven for the whole family. She couldn't imagine how horrifying it would have been to hear them throw vile words at each other. But apparently Ridge had seen and heard those words between his parents and he'd done the only thing a child could do under the circumstances. He'd sought out a place where he'd felt safe and at home, with his friend Barry.

He looked at her with skepticism. "Do you? I somehow doubt that you do. When I met your mother I could just tell she'd made things good for her children."

Nicci nodded soberly. "You're right. I grew up in a loving home. But later—" Her features tightened as the memory of those painful years she'd spent with Bill bullied their way into her thoughts. "Well, I don't want to get into that. Just tell me the rest of your story. What happened to you and Barry after you went to boarding school?"

As he absently combed his fingers through Rebel's mane, he said, "When my parents put me in boarding school, I was afraid I'd never get to be with my friend again. But thankfully, Barry's folks realized it was important for us boys to be together and they scraped up enough money to send him to the same boarding school. To this day, I honestly don't know how the Macons' afforded the tuition. Borrowed and made self-sacrifices, I'm sure.

Anyway, I had enough spending money for both me and my friend, so that helped him a little."

Now she had to add generosity to his list of traits. Was the man a genuine golden boy or did she simply want to only see the good in him? While she'd been growing up, her parents had often encouraged her and her siblings to focus on the good in a person. She'd done that with Bill and had failed to see his glaring faults. She couldn't let herself do that a second time.

"So what about college?" she asked. "Was Barry around then?"

Ridge nodded. "For four years. Then he graduated with a degree in agricultural business. He's put that to use helping his father. And me—" He looked at her and shrugged. "Well, you know what I'm doing."

Yes, he was doctoring people with sick hearts, she thought. But Nicolette now understood a little more about this man. He was not only trying to make a place for himself among his peers, he was seeking a home like Barry Macon had shared with him. And deep down, wasn't she? She'd wanted a husband and children so badly. But her chance for that sort of home had been crushed and now the thought of reaching for her dream again was terrifying.

Shoving that bleak thought away, she said, "I think I'd like to meet this childhood friend of yours. He sounds like quite a guy."

Chuckling, he turned a glinting eye on her. "Oh, no. Barry's too much of a flirt to let him loose around you. I'd have to keep him on a leash."

Nicolette laughed lightly to cover the blush that had seeped into her cheeks. "I can handle myself around flirts," she said teasingly. "Is he married?"

"No. He swears I'll be the first one to settle down and have kids."

Trying to hide her curiosity, Nicci cast him a sidelong glance. "Will you?"

His warm brown gaze lingered on her face until her whole body grew hot and uncomfortable.

"I don't know," he said. "I need to find the right woman first."

It was a struggle for Nicci not to urge her horse ahead of him and away from the suggestive look in his eyes and the innuendo in his voice. Flirting lightly with her was something she could handle, anything beyond that was too much for her broken heart to deal with.

"Well, I'm sure you will find her," she said, trying to make her voice as casual as possible. "There are plenty of available women around here who want to get married. Any day the perfect one might walk into the clinic and right into your heart."

Maybe that woman already had walked into his heart, Ridge thought, as he watched Nicci nudge the sorrel on ahead of him. Maybe *she* was the woman who could help him fill his little house with the sound of children and the warmth of love.

But she was a career woman with a job that would hardly allow her time to have a child, much less raise one, he reminded himself. Besides that, she was rich. She wouldn't want to lower her standard of living just to be with him. And if that wasn't enough of a wall between them, she was downright afraid to love again. So why was he here? Why wasn't he out trying to find a woman more suitable to his needs?

Maybe because each time he looked at her, his gut tightened and his heart kicked into high gear. Right or wrong, she affected him in ways no woman ever had. And a suitable mate wasn't what he wanted. He wanted love.

Chapter Six

Twenty minutes down the trail, Nicci and Ridge rode up a gently sloping hill that was veiled with spreading live oaks. The shade was deep and cool and the grass short enough to make sitting on the ground comfortable instead of scratchy.

Both of them tied their mounts to a nearby salt cedar, then carried the saddlebags full of lunch items over a shady spot.

The wind rustled the leaves above their heads and played them like musical chimes. Ridge sighed with pleasure as he looked around him. The slight elevation of the hill gave them a view of the western range, where more Brahmans grazed on vast grassland.

"This is nice. Really beautiful," he murmured with appreciation.

Nicci's gaze followed his. "Well, we could have kept riding until we reached the river. Some of the spots along its banks are very pretty. But we'd have to make a southern detour and it would take us quite a while to reach it."

After making sure there weren't any nearby mounds of fire ants, she dropped her canteen next to the huge tree trunk, then sat cross-legged on the ground.

"There's no need to ride to the river. I like it here," Ridge assured her.

He carefully placed the heavy saddlebags next to the canteen before he joined her on the ground. He leaned his back against the tree trunk and crossed his long legs out in front of him. "All you can hear is the wind in the trees, the birds singing and the locusts buzzing."

"I'm glad you like it."

She reached for the saddlebag full of food and Ridge quickly placed his hand over hers. The touch brought her questioning gaze up to his.

"Thank you, Nicci, for going to all this trouble today," he said gently.

The air between them suddenly sizzled with undercurrents. She glanced away from him and the open pleasure on his face. "It's no trouble," she said huskily.

Even though his hand was lying lightly over hers, it felt like a hot iron, making her acutely aware of his callused palm, the heat of his body and the small space separating the two of them.

"Remember, Nicci, I'm a doctor. I know how rare it is to have free time for anything. You probably had a thousand things you'd rather be doing than riding with me around your ranch."

There were probably a thousand things she *should* be doing, Nicci told herself, other than sitting here with this man who made her heart thump just a bit too hard and fast. But if she was going to be totally honest with herself, she knew being here with him was the *only* thing she wanted to do.

"Don't worry about it. I like to ride whenever I have the chance." She carefully eased her hand from beneath his and quickly dug several sandwiches from the leather pouch. "Uh, looks like Cook has made roast beef, tuna or bologna. Which would you like to start with?"

He took off his hat and ran a hand through his flattened hair. Finger-combed strands fell across his forehead.

"Give me a beef," he told her.

She handed him the sandwich and a small bag of chips, then took the same for herself. As she began to eat, she tried her best to ignore his nearness, but it was almost impossible to do when his thigh was only inches from hers and each time he made the slightest move his upper arm brushed her shoulder. Every nerve ending inside of her seemed to be awake and ready to jump at his slightest touch.

"When did the Sandbur first originate?" he asked after they'd both taken a few bites. "Did your family start the ranch?"

Glad to have something other than him to focus her thoughts on, Nicci nodded. "My great-great-grandparents, Sylas and Amalia Ketchum, started this place sometime around 1900. When Sylas passed away in 1936 during the Depression, the ownership went to his son, Nate, and Nate's wife, Sara. Once they died, the ranch was then handed on to my mother and her sister, Elizabeth."

He looked impressed. "So your family has owned this land for more than a hundred years. That's quite a legacy."

Her family roots were deep in Texas soil, going back to when it was the Republic of Texas. Throughout the years, one generation of Ketchums had passed a legacy on to the next. It was a fact she was proud of and yet at times it saddened her to think she had no child to continue the tradition.

"Yes," she agreed. "But there have been times when the Sandbur wasn't always prosperous. During the Great Depression my grandfather sold some parts just to have enough money to hold the rest together. But later, Sara, my grandmother came into oil royalties and that pretty much saved things. Nate bought back the old property, and the Sandbur returned to its original size."

He glanced at her as he popped a potato chip into his mouth. "Sounds like your family are fighters. What about your dad? I haven't heard you mention him. Is he still living?"

With a wistful shake of her head, she said, "My father's name was Paul. He was killed about ten years ago in a boating accident. At least, the police called it an accident. We're not really sure what happened. He supposedly went overboard while fishing with some friends down on the gulf."

Regret filled his eyes. "That's too bad, Nicci. You and your family must have been crushed. Was he a cattleman, too?"

Thoughts of her loving father still had the power to sadden her, and she looked down at her half-eaten sandwich and willed away the lump in her throat. "He knew his way around a ranch and helped with the cattle when he was needed, but he made his own mark working as an engineer for an oil company in San Antonio. I miss him terribly. He was a wonderful father."

"I'm sure," he murmured gently, then posed the question, "I guess your mother never remarried?"

Sighing, Nicci tried to swallow down another bite of sandwich. The ball of bread and meat seemed to scratch its way to her stomach. "No. She's interested. But I guess Daddy is a hard act to follow. She's very particular about men."

A dimple came and went in one of his cheeks. "You mean, sort of like her daughter?"

Even though she realized he was mostly teasing, her mouth popped open. She'd never thought of herself in that light and the revelation surprised her.

"I'm not particular about men," she answered after a moment. "I just mainly avoid them."

He balled up the plastic wrap that had covered his sandwich and shoved it into an empty section of the saddlebag.

"You're not avoiding me," he pointed out.

There was no need for him to remind her that he was a man, Nicci thought helplessly. There hadn't been a second that ticked by since he'd arrived on the ranch when she'd forgotten his potent presence. And now that the two of them were alone, everything about him seemed magnified.

Glancing away from his tempting face, she said, "I—you're here as a friend. That's all."

"Hmm. Funny, but I don't feel exactly like a…friend."

The low purring sound of his voice was a warning, and Nicci turned her head just in time to see his upper body leaning toward hers.

"I invited you out here to see the ranch," she quickly reminded him. "Nothing more."

As Nicci watched a slow smile lift the corners of his lips, she felt the air drain from her lungs, her heart leap into a fast jig. She'd never been this close to a man like him, who oozed charm and sexuality, and her senses were quickly turning traitor.

"And I came here to see the ranch because it's your home," he admitted. "Nothing more."

She forced herself to breathe and tried to resist the invisible pull of his body. "If you think I'm—"

He cut her off by lifting his hand to her cheek. His eyes narrowed sensually as he moved the tips of his fingers over her soft skin. "Right now I think you're the most irresistible woman I've ever met."

Her head managed to move slightly to one side and then the other. "Not hardly." She gestured down to her jeans and boots. "Not looking like this."

His fingers stopped their travels across her cheek to cup the side of her face. "Especially like this, Nicci."

A yearning, soft and sweet, billowed up in her and clouded her senses. Her gray eyes connected with his brown ones, and the tender light she saw there tugged on her heart and, just for a moment, made it forget all the scars and walls surrounding it.

"Ridge, don't—do this," she choked out desperately.

His face dipped closer and he whispered

against her lips, "Do what? Show you how attracted I am to you? What's wrong with that?"

A tiny, helpless groan sounded in the back of her throat. "You're—wasting your time."

"Let me judge that for myself," he told her, then promptly proceeded to fasten his lips over hers.

Even in her dazed state, Nicci realized he wasn't holding her captive. At any time, she could pull away and end the kiss. That is, if she had the strength to resist. But his touch left her as weak as a puppy. She couldn't think of ending anything when everything about his hard lips was drawing her closer, reminding her just how hungry she was for this contact with him.

As the search of his lips deepened, he removed the hat from her head. Somewhere in the back of Nicci's mind, she sensed him tossing the crumpled straw to one side. Then his arms came around her and he was dragging her against the hard length of his body.

Nicci didn't try to stop the forward motion that had her falling into the seductive circle of his arms. Being this close to him was like getting a peek into heaven. She couldn't refuse the incredible pleasure his mouth was giving hers. She couldn't deny her body the sweetness of having Ridge's hard muscles next to it.

As soon as the first kiss ended another one began. Before either of them realized what was happening, he was kissing her over and over, and Nicci was responding, clinging to him out of pure need.

The fire that had started out as a flicker in her lower belly was rapidly growing to an all-consuming flame, and she couldn't resist when his hand delved beneath the hem of her blouse and cupped one breast.

A soft sigh escaped her as his plundering mouth moved downward to the tender slope of her neck and on to the delicate skin exposed by the opening of her blouse. Her fingers clamped into the muscles of his shoulders and her head fell invitingly back against his arm.

Sometime during the embrace her hair had come loose from its braid. Ridge ran his fingers through the silky brown waves as he lifted his head and smiled at her with his lips and his eyes.

"Sweetheart, that didn't feel like I was wasting my time at all," he said, his voice husky with desire.

His observation was a jarring reminder to Nicci that she'd fallen under his spell and in doing so had given him all the wrong signals.

Quickly, before this thing between them got totally out of hand, she scrambled out of his arms and shot to her feet.

Dazed by the abrupt separation, Ridge watched her turn her back and walk to the far edge of the live oak's shade. Once she stopped, she tossed her head and her long brown hair rippled like a piece of satin against her back. Her stance was rigid, her hands clenched at her sides. Even from this distance he could feel the tension in her body, and the knowledge that she regretted kissing him tore a hole right through the center of his chest.

Slowly he rose to his feet and walked up behind her. The contact of his hands on her shoulders caused her to flinch, but rather than turn and face him, she continued to stare out at the open range sweeping miles toward the western horizon.

Bringing his cheek to rest against the side of her head, Ridge murmured, "I'm sorry if I've upset you, Nicci. That wasn't my intention."

That brought her whole body around. She

looked at him with woeful gray eyes. "It doesn't matter what your intentions were, Ridge. I'm not interested. And that—what just happened a moment ago—can't be repeated. We're either going to be friends or—nothing at all."

His mouth a grim line, he studied her bitter face.

"Is that the way you kiss all your friends, Nicci? Or am I the only privileged one?"

Bright pink color washed up her throat and covered her face. "You—you caught me off guard. So don't start feeling proud of yourself, Dr. Garroway."

The corners of his lips lifted in a faint, perceptive smile. "You wanted those kisses, Nicci. Maybe you can make yourself believe otherwise. But you won't make me believe anything else. I felt the need in your hands. The hunger on your lips."

"Shut up," she muttered fiercely.

"Why? Because you can't bear to think that you might need a man, that you might actually be human?"

Her eyes clouded over and her head swung slowly back and forth. "Why are you trying to hurt me like this, Ridge?"

Groaning with disbelief, he cradled her

face in his hands. "Oh, Nicci, I'm not trying to hurt you. I'm trying to make you see that there's something special between us. I felt it the first moment I saw you. And I think you feel it, too. You just don't want to admit it. Why don't you want to give us a chance?"

The earnest light in his eyes was like a beacon, tempting her to reach out, to let herself feel the pleasure of being in his arms, to think of a future with him at her side. But she was wise enough to know she couldn't give in to the allure of his charms. Jumping into a relationship with Ridge would ultimately be more painful than jumping into a pit of fire. Even if she did survive the flames, she'd be scarred for life.

In a plaintive voice she said, "Because it would be all wrong, Ridge. That's why. It would never work."

Before he could utter a protest, she pulled away and walked back to the tree trunk where they'd been sitting.

With quick, deliberate movements, she gathered the remains of their lunch.

Ridge walked to where she stood. "What are you doing? I wasn't finished with lunch."

"You are now," she quipped.

Not about to be deterred, he took the saddlebag from her and sat back down at the base of the tree trunk.

With her hands jammed on either side of her hips, she watched him pull out another sandwich and begin to eat as though he had the whole day to waste.

"We need to go," she said. "It's a long ride back to the ranch yard. And I—"

"We're not going anywhere, Nicci," he interrupted. "Until you sit down here beside me and give me a good reason why the two of us can't be…more than friends."

His casual attitude infuriated her. It also made her see that she might as well get the issue over and done with. Otherwise, he might sit there till nightfall, and she couldn't go back to the ranch without him. For one thing, the trail they'd followed branched off in many directions. He might not know the way back. Secondly, if she showed up at the Saddler house without Ridge, it would be worse than embarrassing for both of them.

With a sigh of surrender, she took a seat on the ground, but made sure she was safely out of his reach.

"I don't know why I need to spell this out to you, Ridge. You're an intelligent man. The reasons ought to be clear."

He looked at her squarely, and the touch of his gaze on her face only reminded her of her loose hair and bare lips and the reckless way she'd behaved in his arms.

"Indulge me," he said simply.

Damn it, why did he have to look so young, so good, she wondered. Up until now, keeping men out of her life had been easy. Ridge was changing all that.

Licking her lips, she turned her head to one side and focused her gaze on a honeybee buzzing around a thicket of wild roses. Probably one of those male drones whose only job was to keep his queen happy, she thought dryly.

"I'm nine years older than you, Ridge. That might not seem like a great distance to you. But it is. In a few years I'll be an old woman, while you'll still be a young, virile man."

Amusement dimpled his cheeks as he shook his head. "You're gonna have to do better than that, Nicci."

Her lips clamped together as she drew in a deep, bracing breath. "Have you always wanted to date a grandmother?" she asked tartly.

Laughter rumbled from deep in his chest and she couldn't miss the twinkle in his eyes.

"One that looks like you."

Rolling her eyes toward the heavy swag of limbs just above their heads, she said, "I won't always look this way."

"Beauty isn't youth or the number on a calendar, Nicci."

His remark caught her off guard and she realized yet again that he was definitely not the man she'd first thought him to be. He was far more dangerous, because he was beginning to touch her on the inside where she was most vulnerable.

"Okay," she said, trying to cling to her practical side. "I'll give you more to think about than our age difference. I've gone through the dating game. I've been through a marriage. I don't want any part of either of them again. Is that plain enough?"

Ridge started to tell her that her kisses had contradicted her words, but he kept the remark to himself. Now wasn't the time to push her. Not when he could see shadows of sadness in her eyes. The last thing he wanted was to anger or hurt her. He wanted to take those shadows away. He wanted to hear her laugh, see her smile. Most of all, he wanted her to reach out to him because her heart compelled her to.

Smiling gently, he said, "All right, Nicci. I won't push you anymore about the matter. At least, not today."

But he would later. The unspoken words hung between them, and for a moment Nicci was tempted to tell him about her marriage to Bill, how he'd lied about wanting children, how he'd continued to deceive her for years with empty promises, and how in the end he'd turned to other women and taken pleasure in flaunting them in her face. Maybe if she told him all of that, he would understand her fears, her reluctance to feel anything toward a man again.

But she couldn't tell him those things. The past was still too painful for her heart to confess. And she didn't want him to know that a man had so easily duped her, that she'd blindly loved and trusted instead of seeing reality. After all, she was supposed to be a smart woman and that's how she wanted Ridge to think of her.

"Here," he said, as he took the cup from a metal thermos and poured a small amount of coffee into it. "I promise to be your obedient slave for the rest of the day. So let's have dessert and enjoy the rest of our ride. Okay?"

Just seeing the dimples on his face was

enough to melt Nicci like butter on a hot biscuit. After a moment's consideration she decided there couldn't be any harm in being with him for the remainder of the day. As long as she remembered their time together was temporary, it wouldn't hurt to let herself dream a little.

He handed her the coffee, and as she sipped, she smiled at him over the rim. "Sure, Ridge."

Chapter Seven

Three days later, Nicci was sitting in her office, preparing to deal with an afternoon barrage of patients. Several medical charts lay on her desktop, but she'd not yet read over the details of any of them. Instead she was gazing out the window overlooking the city park that ran adjacent to the clinic's parking lot.

The day was hot, with only a few harmless puffs of clouds to mar the bright-blue sky. Young children were running and playing on the green grass, swinging on the swing sets and sliding down a tall, curved slide. Mothers were among them, guiding, soothing and watching over their young sons and daughters.

Her eyes wistful, Nicci remembered back to when she'd first told her parents she was getting married. She'd happily promised to give them a houseful of grandchildren and she'd walked down the church aisle believing she was stepping toward the family of her dreams. Instead, each year had passed with her parents wishing and hoping and wondering when their daughter would become pregnant. Nicolette had also hoped and prayed for even one child to come into her life.

At that time she'd not known it was medically impossible for Bill to have children. His surgery to become sterilized had been just another one of his cruel deceptions and one she'd not discovered until the end of their bitter marriage. By then her father had died and she was almost glad he'd not been around to see her utter failure.

Sighing at the heaviness in her heart, she turned away from the window and picked up the chart lying atop the tall stack in front of her. Now wasn't the time to be wallowing in disappointment, she fiercely told herself.

Maybe it wasn't meant for her to be a mother, but she still had a rich life with her job and her friends. She was blessed. She shouldn't be wishing for more.

Nicci opened the chart and began to scan a battery of test results. She'd hardly reached the bottom of the page when Jacki, her assistant, walked through the door carrying a massive bouquet of yellow roses interspersed with delicate baby's breath.

Staring with surprise, Nicci asked, "Where did those come from?"

The nurse placed the vase on a bare spot of Nicci's desk, then with a sly smile, pointed to the card pinned to a blue ribbon. "I don't know. You tell me."

Nicci's brows shot up. "You mean the roses are for me?"

Jacki laughed with disbelief. "Well surely you know they're not for me. I don't know anybody who could afford two dozen roses like these. Besides, that's your name on the front of the card."

Nicci couldn't remember the last time she'd gotten roses. Years ago, she supposed, before Bill had quit being her husband.

She stared at the flowers, her mind spinning to the doctor at the opposite end of the building. The bouquet had to be from Ridge. But why? Even though they'd had a nice ride over the ranch last Saturday, and a lovely dinner later that evening, she'd made it clear to him that she didn't want to become romantically involved. And he'd accepted her feelings on the matter. At least, she'd thought he'd accepted them. She'd not heard from him or seen him since his visit to the Sandbur.

Standing near the corner of the desk, Jacki impatiently tapped her foot. "Well, aren't you going to look? Or is this a secret or something?"

Not wanting her assistant to think she was hiding anything, Nicolette unpinned the card with fumbling fingers and opened the envelope. After she read the short message, she folded it and glanced at Jacki.

"The roses are to thank me for dinner last Saturday night. And he wants to return the favor by cooking dinner for me at his place."

"The good doctor." Jacki's blue eyes suddenly gleamed with excitement. "You're going to accept his invitation, aren't you?"

Releasing a long breath, Nicolette thrust the small square of paper back into the envelope. "I really shouldn't, Jacki. It would only encourage him."

Jacki rolled her eyes. "Duh! Isn't that what any normal, hot-blooded woman would do? Nicolette, the man is sexy as sin and on top of that he seems nice. What more do you want?"

Rising from her desk, Nicolette adjusted her lab coat, then picked up the patient chart she'd been reading. She couldn't let herself think about what she wanted. At one time in her life she'd wanted a lot of things, desperately, but in the end, all she'd gotten for it were bitter memories.

"I don't *want* anything, Jacki. Except my work. That's enough for me. More than enough."

"You're lying."

If Jacki hadn't been a friend, Nicci would have reprimanded her. But instead Nicci simply scowled at her.

"I'm not lying. And I'm not hot-blooded. Believe me, Jacki, Bill turned my blood to chunks of ice."

Grimacing, Jacki said, "Yeah, but I'm betting Dr. Garroway can melt it."

He could melt it all right, Nicolette thought. Just the memory of his kisses was enough to turn her face scarlet. For the past three days she'd been trying to forget those moments in the shade of the live oak tree. But try as she might, she couldn't push away the excitement Ridge's kisses had shot through her that afternoon. The memories wedged their way into her thoughts, and though she knew spending that time in his arms had been reckless, she didn't regret it.

For the first time in years, the future had begun to sneak into Nicci's thoughts and in it she was thinking of herself as a woman again, imagining herself with a second chance at love. Dreaming those sorts of dreams was probably leading her toward heartache. But Ridge had scrambled her senses.

Sighing, she glanced back at the beautiful roses on her desk. Just what was he trying to say and should she even care?

Biting down on her lower lip, she turned her gaze back to Jacki. "I do enjoy being with the man. He's nice and fun. But I'm afraid he has more than friendship on his mind."

A giggle erupted from the red-haired nurse. "Nicci, look at yourself! Of course he has more than friendship on his mind. The man would be crazy if he didn't!"

Shaking her head, Nicolette said, "Jacki,

Dr. Garroway is a young, good-looking man. He could have his pick of women. And frankly, I can't understand his attraction to me."

"You always underestimate yourself, Nicci. And you always just think of yourself as a...doctor," she finished with a frustrated groan.

"That's what I am, Jacki," Nicolette retorted. "And I'm not in the market for a brief affair with Dr. Garroway."

She marched toward the door with the intention of heading to one of the examining rooms. Jacki followed quickly on her heels.

"Maybe the doctor doesn't want an affair, Nicci. Maybe he's thinking in longer terms."

Jacki's comments had Nicolette pausing at the door and turning her head back to her friend.

"Are you suggesting that Ridge might be thinking of marriage?"

With a totally innocent smile, Jacki nodded. "It's possible, isn't it?"

A disbelieving laugh rolled past Nicolette's lips. "Never."

Impatient now, Jacki shook a finger at her. "Are you certain? I dare you to prove me wrong."

Nicolette shot her a droll look. "And how do you expect me to do that? Ask him his intentions? Not in a million years."

Jacki scowled at her. "You can start by accepting his invitation to dinner. Instead of running like a scared rabbit."

Did she really want to find out what he wanted, Nicolette asked herself. She wasn't sure. However, she was certain she needed to see him again. Good or bad, she didn't want to end everything between them.

She turned toward examining room three with Jacki at her side. "All right. All right," she muttered under her breath. "When we finish with Mr. Pendleton, I'll walk down to Ridge's office and tell him to put the skillet on. I wouldn't want you thinking I'm a chicken or anything like that."

Smiling smugly, Jacki said, "Oh no. Never."

A few minutes later, Nicolette walked to the other side of the busy medical clinic. Ridge's waiting room was full of patients, but after a quick call, the receptionist invited Nicolette to step back to his private office.

When Nicolette knocked lightly on the closed door and entered the small room,

Ridge was sitting at his desk. But the moment he spotted her, he rose to his feet and hurried toward her.

"Nicci! You've surprised me!"

A broad smile lit his face as he reached for both her hands and clasped them in his.

Even if Nicolette's resistance had been made of iron, his touch would have smelted it like a red-hot forge. Seeing his happy face again lifted her heart like nothing else could. In spite of all the reservations going through her mind, she felt herself smiling back at him.

"Hello, Ridge. I'm sorry to interrupt your work. It's obvious you're very busy. Your waiting room is stuffed."

There was a sparkle to his brown eyes as they roamed her face. "Don't worry about it. My patients would all go into cardiac arrest if they didn't have to wait for me."

She chuckled softly, then, clearing her throat, she eased her hands from his grip. "Uh, thank you for the roses. They're incredibly beautiful."

His fingers reached up to touch her cheek. "Not nearly as beautiful as you."

The thought that she should be scolding him raced through Nicolette's mind, but just as quickly, she pushed that thought away. She'd chosen to be here, even while knowing he wanted more than a platonic relationship with her. In showing up at his office, she'd crossed an invisible line and moved to a place where she couldn't turn around or back up. All she could do now was face him and wait to see what happened.

The idea was terrifying, but then so was the notion of sitting at home or in her office tortured with what-ifs and loneliness.

Swallowing away the lump that had suddenly thickened her throat, she said, "I also wanted to thank you for the dinner invitation. When do you plan to do all this cooking?" Then she teased him with hopes of lightening the moment. "And will it be safe to eat?"

He chuckled and she could see from the look on his face that she'd made him a happy man. The thought empowered her and left her feeling so bubbly she wanted to laugh out loud.

"Tonight. Seven o'clock. And trust me, Nicci. It may not be quite as good as one of Cook's meals, but in my next life I'll be a gourmet chef."

Her eyes widened. "Seven tonight! I have a late appointment this evening, Ridge. I don't know if I can make it out to the ranch to change and then back to your place by then."

His hands cupped her shoulders before they slid lightly down her arms. "You don't need to change," he insisted. "Besides, you don't know where I live. I'll wait for you to finish up here at the clinic and then we'll go together."

Shaking her head, she said, "That's too much trouble."

"No trouble at all. I've got plenty of work right here." He gestured to his desk. "When you finish up, just walk down here. Okay?"

Feeling a reckless excitement she hadn't felt since she was a teenager, she nodded. "I'll try not to be too late."

She turned to leave and he quickly caught her by the hand. She looked around in question to see the teasing sparkle in his eyes had faded to a simmering glow. A shiver of anticipation slipped down her spine.

"Just in case you didn't know, Nicci, you've made me very happy."

But for how long, she wondered. Hours? A day? A week? Or would this thing that was budding between them turn out to be something more lasting, like Jacki had suggested? No. Nicci wouldn't dare let herself think in those terms. For now she would think of Ridge Garroway as a one-evening event.

"I have patients waiting, too. I'll see you later," she said, and hurried out of his office.

Hours later, Ridge was sitting at his desk, plowing through a mound of paperwork while he waited for Nicolette, when his cell phone rang.

Seeing the caller was his mother, he almost didn't answer. He was in a good mood and he wanted to stay that way. But with Nicolette having dinner with him tonight, he didn't want to be bothered with the phone continually ringing. And, if anything, his mother was persistent. She'd dial repeatedly until he answered.

"Hello, Mom."

"Ridge, honey, I was beginning to get worried!" she wailed in pitiful relief. "You haven't answered my calls all day."

He could hear the faint slur of alcohol in her voice, but that was nothing new for Lillian Garroway. Where most people looked to a hobby for relief and relaxation, she turned to gin or vodka. In all his twenty-nine years, he'd never seen his mother in a state of intoxication, but there had been times she'd come damn close. The most prominent image Ridge had of his mother was her wandering listlessly through the house with a cocktail in one hand and a cigarette in the other. He hated the fact that she was wasting precious hours and days, not to mention the physical damage she was doing to her body. But she seemed bent on ruining the very things she'd been blessed with.

"I'm a doctor, Mom. There are times when it's impossible for me to answer the phone."

She let out an exaggerated sigh. "Yes, yes, I know. I've heard all the excuses before."

Realizing he sounded like his own father, he grimaced as he tossed down the ink pen and leaned back in his chair.

"Sorry, Mom. It's just that I've had a busy day. I wasn't trying to ignore you."

She sniffed. "Well, I wouldn't blame you if you did. I'm not exactly a barrel of laughs these days. What with you gone, I don't have much to look forward to."

Ridge silently groaned. "You have everything to look forward to. You just need to wake up and realize it."

"How? I don't have a husband. Not really. And my son has moved to the ends of the earth. This house is like a tomb. Ivy slips through the rooms like some damn ghost. She's scared me so many times, I've threatened to put a bell around her neck."

Ivy was the longtime Garroway housekeeper. Over the years the woman had become more of a caretaker than anything. She handled everything in the household that his mother wasn't capable of coping with, which was becoming most everything. Ridge was amazed the woman had the constitution to deal with Lillian on a daily basis.

"You need to get out of there, Mom, do something productive. It will make you feel better."

"Are you giving me advice as a doctor or as my son?" she asked with sarcasm.

"Both." He glanced at his watch and wondered how much longer it would be before Nicolette showed up. Soon, he hoped. He didn't want to start the evening being dragged down by his mother's sour attitude.

"Well, I don't have anything to do right now," she whined. "Except pick out a dress for the mayor's inaugural ball. And I don't have the heart for that. Not with all this weight around my waist."

Ridge closed his eyes and breathed deeply.

Lillian had never known how to talk to a son. He wasn't sure she knew how to have a meaningful exchange of words with anyone. Her conversations always began and ended with personal pronouns. I, me, my. Those were her favorite subjects. But perhaps that was because she was so hungry for attention, he thought sadly. Ridge's father, Richard, had never really treated Lillian as a wife. She was more like a possession he could put away or take out according to his whims.

That idea had his thoughts suddenly turning to Nicolette and the members of her family he'd had the pleasure of meeting at the Sandbur dinner. Even though they were a wealthy family, they were all hard working, compassionate people. True, they were obviously ambitious, but they were motivated by love and devotion to keeping the legacy of their ancestors going. Greed didn't fit into their thinking.

If only the Garroways had followed a more humble trail, he thought wistfully.

To his mother he said, "I've encouraged you to join a gym. It would be a good way to deal with your weight and, at the same time, get you out of the house. And as for something to do, I've invited you to come visit my home."

She let out a laugh that was both nervous and mocking. "Home! Ridge, honey, that place isn't your home. From what you've told me it's little more than a shack. Do you honestly think I want to see you in those conditions?"

"I do have indoor plumbing, Mom."

"Okay, go ahead and make light of the situation. But we both know your home is here in Houston. And it's high time you got yourself back here!"

Leaning forward in the chair, Ridge propped his elbows on the edge of the desk. "Sorry, Mom. That's not going to happen. I'm sinking roots here."

A snort blasted his ear. "Roots, hell! The Garroways have always had their place in this city. Your daddy's great-great ancestors moved here from Virginia when Texas was still a republic and they've never left Houston soil! They made their mark here! Except you," she said with pointed accusation, then added wearily, "God knows I'd have to be the one to sire a deserter. Richard certainly never lets me forget it."

Having any sort of meaningful relationship with Richard, his father, had ended long ago when the elder Garroway had realized his son was not going to follow directly in his footsteps. Now the two of them traded little more than cool hellos.

Struggling to push down the dark resentment he harbored toward the man, Ridge said, "I'm sorry you and Dad feel the way you do. But I'm a doctor and we're supposed to go where we're needed. With Dr. Walters retiring, this town needed another cardiologist. And I'm here to serve the people."

"Serve the people!" She was practically yelling now. "If you're going to stay in that Podunk town you might as well go into missionary work. And for what? When you could be in an elite circle here. You'd be making real money. And your father could hold his head up with pride."

Ridge's teeth clamped together. He loved his mother, but there were times he couldn't abide her views or her behavior.

"Unlike my father and grandfather, I'm not in this for the money," he clipped coolly.

"Hmmph!" She let out another cynical snort. "Since when did you become so righteous?"

"I don't know," he said with all honesty. "But thankfully, somewhere along the way, I was blessed with a spark of decency. Maybe you ought to pray for a little yourself, Mother.

In the meantime if you want to see me I've given you my address. The door will be open."

There was a long pause, and Ridge knew she was thinking over all that she'd just said to him. And more than likely she was already regretting half of her words. But that was Lillian. She always spoke before using her mind.

"Ridge, I—"

"I've got to go, Mom," he wearily interrupted. "I'll talk to you later."

He shut off the phone and slipped it into his pocket. With the phone call out of the way, he tried to focus on the waiting paperwork, but his mother's words had stirred things inside of him that wouldn't let him rest.

Shoving the papers to one side of his desk, he rose from his chair with the intention of leaving the office. A light knock sounded on the door.

Before he could respond, Nicolette stuck her head around the wooden panel. "Here I am, finally," she announced. "Are you ready to go?"

The sight of her smiling face was just what he needed to put his world back on its axis, and as Ridge hurried over to her, he realized with each day that passed, she was becoming more and more important to him.

"More than ready," he said as he joined her out in the hallway. "Just let me lock up and we'll be on our way."

Moments later, after he'd secured his office and the outer door leading to the waiting area, the two of them exited the building.

The evening was still terribly warm with hardly a breeze to stir the humid air. Nicolette's brown hair was coiled and fastened to the back of her head with a tortoiseshell clamp, but the tendrils framing her face had turned into damp corkscrews. A straight khaki skirt with a slit up one side exposed a glimpse of shapely thigh, while her white shirt with the sleeves rolled up was buttoned just low enough to tease him with a glimpse of cleavage. She managed to look both prim and sensual at the same time.

"I'm glad you didn't go home to change," he said, as he settled his arm against the back of her waist. "You look very sexy tonight. I'm just wondering, though, about the poor male patients you saw today. The sight of you must have sent their blood pressure skyrocketing."

She scoffed at his compliment with soft laughter. "None of my patients saw me like this. I was covered with a lab coat."

"Good," he purred. "I wouldn't want any of the men to get ideas about my girl."

By now they had reached his pickup truck and she looked up at him with wary speculation. "Your girl, huh? Where did you get that idea?"

Smiling, he dug the key out of his pocket and punched the automatic locking system. "You're here with me. That gives me a little hint."

He opened the door and gestured for her to get in. She looked at him with raised brows.

"I'm going to drive my car and follow you," she told him.

He shook his head. "No. I'll bring you back later to get your car. It will be fine here in the parking lot."

Nicolette didn't argue. There were two very capable security men who patrolled the building and parking lot. She wouldn't worry about her vehicle. And it would be nice to rest from the day's work before she had to deal with traffic.

"All right," she agreed. "But this is a lot of trouble for you."

He offered her a hand up into the passenger's seat. "Don't start thinking of me as nice," he said with a teasing grin. "I'm really selfish, Nicci. I'd do anything to have you with me this evening."

She took his hand and he brushed a quick kiss on her cheek as he helped her into the cab. With a silent groan, Nicolette watched him skirt the hood and take his seat behind the wheel. How could she possibly act her age, when he was so young and full of life? Everything about him pulled her spirits into a joyful skip. When she was with him she didn't want to be wise or serious. She wanted to laugh and feel the blood humming through her veins.

"Well, actually, I was going to turn down your invitation. But Jacki, my assistant, talked me into this," she admitted.

He started the engine before casting her a look that held amusement crossed with a dash of censure. "Three cheers to Jacki. But why weren't you going to accept? Or should I even ask?"

Crossing her legs, she tugged at the slit on her skirt. Any other day she would have worn a safe, sedate pair of slacks. Instead, she'd gone for coolness, and now bare skin was showing everywhere.

"You should know enough about me now, Ridge, to know that I usually like to play things safe. And spending time with you is definitely not safe."

One brow arched above his brown eyes, and she watched a dimple come and go in his cheek. Dear Lord, he was too much for any woman's senses to deal with.

"Hmm. I like the sound of that," he drawled. "A man never wants a woman to consider him as safe. I must be doing something right."

Something right? He was doing everything right. And she was falling into his hands like a ripe peach just waiting to be eaten. How soon would it be before he gobbled up her heart?

Chapter Eight

Once they departed the parking lot, Ridge drove south until they reached Rio Grande Street, then he turned west until they crossed the Guadalupe River and hit the highway heading toward Goliad. They were just leaving the river bottom, when he turned south again on a farm-to-market road. On either side of the blacktop road, the flat fields were green with knee-high cotton that was presently in full white bloom.

The farmland went for several miles before the scenery returned to cattle grazing among the mesquite and wesatch bushes.

"Are we there yet?" she teased.

"Actually, we are. See that corner post right there? That's where my property starts."

Her gaze followed the direction of his pointing finger. The barbed wire fence was sagging, but the posts were still upright and the H braces intact. She didn't see any cattle, but since he'd told her he owned two hundred acres, the animals could be elsewhere.

"I'm still just getting things going," he warned. "So don't expect too much."

Smiling, she tried to assure him. "Ridge, I'm not a critical person. My staff says I'm a perfectionist only because I demand the best care for my patients. Outside of that, I don't expect everything to be perfect."

A faint look of relief crossed his face. "I'm glad. 'Cause you're definitely not going to see another Sandbur."

Feeling the need to reassure him, she reached over and gently touched his forearm. "I don't want to see another Sandbur, Ridge. I want to see *your* home."

That place isn't your home. From what you've told me it's little more than a shack.

His mother's words sounded in his ears, and though he quickly shoved them away, he couldn't help but wonder if Nicolette's rich background would have her seeing his property in the same judgmental way. He didn't want to believe she was in the same league as his parents. But then, he'd been fooled before. Especially where Brittany was concerned. When he'd first met her, he believed a place like this was her heart's desire, especially if the two of them were sharing it together. It had taken a hard slap of reality to make him see she was all about herself.

"We're almost there," he said.

When Ridge turned into the short drive leading up to the house, Nicolette leaned eagerly forward in the plush bucket seat.

On first glance, she could tell the house had been built in the 1930s or 40s. At some time during the years, the outside had been covered with planked cedar. The boards were now weathered to a soft pewter gray that contrasted gracefully with the blue metal roof. Porches were attached to the front and west side of the house, both of which were deep enough to hold several groups of outdoor furniture.

As they grew closer, Nicolette could see the yard was shaded with a huge pecan tree, along with several live oaks and Mexican palms. Crimson bougainvillea climbed rampantly up the post supporting the porch, while dark-yellow lantana grew thick against the latticework underpinning. St. Augustine grass spread lush and green across the deeply shaded lawn.

Surprise marked her face when she finally looked over at him. "I don't know what to say, Ridge. This is—nothing like I expected."

His face stoic, he braked the truck to a stop outside the yard fence and killed the engine. Turning toward her, he asked in a guarded tone, "What were you expecting, Nicci? I warned you that it needed work."

Frowning that he was so quick to misinterpret her words, she said, "I don't mean that! I meant that I never expected it to look this homey or beautiful!" Fumbling quickly with her seat belt, she pushed it aside and reached to open the door. "Come on. I want to see everything!"

Before he could walk around and help her out of the vehicle, Nicci slid to the ground and hurried over to the low board fence surrounding the yard. As he joined her, she sighed with appreciation.

"The shade is so deep and cool."

He said, "I figure the pecan tree has to be at least two hundred years old."

Nodding, she lifted her gaze to the lofty branches. "I'll bet that old tree has seen a lot in its time." She leveled her gaze back on the yard and the area behind the house. Excitement filled her voice when she spotted a small, rickety shed. "Is that an old chicken house I see?"

"It is. I've purchased lumber to repair it. But that's going to come after the fence building. Keeping the cattle and horses on my own property is my first priority," he told her, then looked at her with dry skepticism. "Don't tell me you know something about chickens."

She shot him an offended look. "I know all about them. We used to have a chicken coop out behind the ranch house. Cook kept about two-dozen dominicker hens and I would help her gather the eggs."

He moved a fraction closer and Nicolette was sure she could feel the heat of his body arcing into hers. In days past she would have casually eased away from him and the temptation he evoked. But she was growing addicted to the excitement he stirred in her. So much so that when she was away from him, she yearned to see his face, feel his touch and hear the husky drawl of his voice. It was as if Ridge had turned back the years for her and she'd reverted to a teenage girl who sighed with longing for the boy next door.

"You don't have the chickens anymore?" he asked.

His question interrupted her thoughts and she shook her head. "Not anymore. The eggs attracted snakes of all kinds. Cook used to carry a shotgun with her when we'd enter the chicken house, just in case. We tried keeping cats around, but they would always run off to the barn. Guess the idea of fat rats was more inviting to them than snakes. My father was always afraid one of us kids would reach into a nest and pick up a rattlesnake instead of an egg. He said he'd rather buy eggs from the store. So we got rid of the chickens."

His hand curled around her upper arm, and Nicolette matched her steps to his as he guided her toward a small gate that would let them into the front yard.

"I don't want snakes around, either. But I doubt I'll get my wishes. I've had a few locals warn me that rattlesnakes are bad in this area," he remarked. "I'm hoping Enoch will keep them chased away."

As the two of them walked up a beaten

grassy path toward the porch, his hand remained on her arm. His fingers warmed her flesh and sent sparks of awareness circuiting through her body. Trying not to dwell on his nearness, she asked, "Who is Enoch?"

"Here he comes right now."

Nicolette followed the direction of his gaze to the east side of the house. A tall, red-haired boy who appeared to be in his early teens was rapidly approaching. At his side was a large German shepherd dog.

"Enoch is the dog," Ridge informed her. "And the fine-looking young man is Corey. He helps me with chores on weekends and after school."

By now the boy was within speaking distance and he held up a hand in greeting. "Hi, Mr. Ridge! I didn't know you were gonna have company this evening."

Nicolette could see the teenager was trying his best to be polite and not stare at her. Apparently he wasn't accustomed to seeing women here at Ridge's place. The notion pleased her. Although, she reminded herself, that even though she was his first female visitor, she probably wouldn't be his last. And she couldn't expect to be the sole woman to share Ridge's personal life. Not when she'd insisted over and over that she wasn't in the market for romance. Still, the idea of him bringing another woman out to this cozy ranch was one she didn't want to consider.

Ridge gestured for Corey to come closer so that he could make introductions. "Nicci, this is Corey, my right-hand man."

The teenager sheepishly ducked his chin. "Shoot, Mr. Ridge, I don't do that much." Through a hank of red hair, he peeped up at Nicolette, then politely stuck out his hand. "Nice to meet you, Miss Nicci."

Smiling, Nicolette shook his hand. "It's nice to meet you, too, Corey. I'll bet you're a big help." Glancing slyly over at Ridge, she asked Corey in a teasing voice, "Is he a good boss?"

"He's the best!" Corey exclaimed. "And he's really good with algebra, too!"

Nicolette arched her brows at Ridge. A faint hint of color swept up his throat and over his jaws. Apparently he wasn't accustomed to being praised in front of others. To look at him, anyone would think he owned the world, or could if he wanted to. Yet she was discovering more and more that he was a practical man without a pretentious bone in his body. When would he ever quit surprising her?

"I'm helping Corey with a summer class," Ridge quickly explained, then, slipping his arm around the back of her waist, he said to Corey, "I'm going to show Nicci around the place before we have supper. Have you fed the horses yet?"

The teenager nodded. "And watered them, too. I'll go spread their hay. Then I'll be finished and out of your way."

The three of them walked across the lawn to the east side of the house. Several yards beyond the fence was a barn with a roof of rusty corrugated iron and sides of bare, weathered lumber. Off to one side of the structure there were two connecting corrals made of iron pipe. In one of the pens a herd of five horses were eating from a wooden feed trough.

Nicolette turned her gaze to Corey. "You don't have to hurry away on my account. I'm sure Ridge can cook enough for three."

The warm flicker in Ridge's eyes told Nicolette he appreciated her generous attitude toward the boy. "Sure," he said. "Corey is welcome to stay and eat with us."

"Oh, no!" Corey quickly exclaimed. "If I was to do that my mom would skin me alive! She'd say it was imposin'. But thanks, anyway." With a quick spin on the toe of his tennis shoe, he jogged to the barn. Enoch barked with playful joy and bounded after the boy.

Nicolette smiled wistfully after the two of them. "What a nice boy. And such manners."

Nodding, Ridge said, "I was blessed to have found him. He's not lazy. In fact, he likes to work, even harder than I want him to. And he appreciates everything that I do for him."

"You're acquainted with his parents?" she asked curiously.

"I've talked to his mother a few times after church services. Suzette's a nice, hard-working woman," Ridge told her.

"What about his father?"

Disgust twisted his lips. "Corey doesn't have a father. He walked out on the family when Corey was a baby, and Suzette has never remarried. Guess she's too scared to try again."

Nicolette's jaw tightened briefly as she muttered, "I know the feeling."

Ridge glanced down at her, but didn't comment. Nicolette was glad. She felt too good and too happy to allow herself to think for more than five seconds about Bill and the heartache he'd caused her.

After a moment Ridge went on, "I try to be there for the kid. When he needs to talk about something. Or needs help with his schoolwork. He needs more, though. He needs a father."

The frustration threaded through his voice told Nicolette just how much he cared for Corey. Her heart softened toward the man just that much more. "I can tell by the way he looks at you that you're his hero, Ridge. Don't count short what you're doing for him."

With a faint smile, he urged her toward the barn. "Come on," he said huskily. "Let's go take a look at my horses and you can tell me what you think of them."

Several more minutes passed before the two of them finally entered the house. After Ridge showed her through the simply decorated rooms, they returned to the kitchen, which contained a small dining table, two walls of pine cabinets, a gas cook stove, a new refrigerator and, over the double sink, a wide window that looked out at the pecan tree.

"I'll bet you get a good view of the squirrels from here," Nicolette told him as she stood at the sink and gazed out at the shaded yard. "I wonder if you'll get many pecans? You need to save them to make Christmas goodies. Like pies and pralines."

He was standing a few steps away, shaking salt and pepper and other spices onto two thick steaks. Now he glanced over at her and tried not to dwell on how sexy she looked standing there in the waning light, a bit of thigh showing and her tiny waist nipped in by a wide leather belt.

If Ridge could have his way, he'd forget the food and simply take Nicolette into his arms and carry her to the bedroom. From the moment he'd first met her, he'd been struck with a deep attraction for the woman. But the more he'd gotten to know her, the more that attraction had turned to outright hunger. Especially after those kisses he'd shared with her during the ride on the Sandbur. He couldn't get them, or her, out of his mind, and though he'd been reminding himself to take things slowly everything inside of him wanted to reach out, grab her and never let her go.

"I'll gather the pecans if you'll make the desserts," he offered. "I'm not much of a desert cook. They take a little more finesse than meat and potatoes."

He appeared to be making a permanent

home here so he would probably still be around when Christmas arrived. But would she still be a part of his life, Nicolette wondered. Did she want to be?

Suddenly she was thinking about how it might be to share the task of trimming a Christmas tree with him, to show him how to make fudge, pumpkin bread and pecan pie. But more than those things, how would it feel, she asked herself, to share the true meaning of Christmas with this man, the gift of love?

For a moment her throat tightened with emotion, and then she jerked her mind out of the pleasant daydreams. It would never do for her to get starry-eyed over Ridge Garroway. He was a good doctor and, more important, he appeared to be a good man. He needed a woman in his life who could come to him with a whole and giving heart. Not a woman who'd already been scarred and jaded.

Moving closer to his side, she tried to focus on the present. "Actually, doctoring puts a crimp in my kitchen time. But I enjoy trying my hand at a few dishes. When did you learn how to cook?"

He switched on a burner beneath a large iron skillet and adjusted the flame. "During my college days. Barry couldn't cook boiled water and neither could I. But I got sick of eating take-out. For a while I thought I was going to turn into a pizza. So I made a trip to the grocery store and learned through trial and error. Believe me, I had more errors than anything. The first time I tried to fry bacon and eggs for breakfast the fire alarm went off."

Nicolette chuckled. "Once I nearly burned the whole kitchen with a grease fire. I didn't realize vegetable oil would ignite if you got it too hot. Anyway, I had to use the fire extinguisher to douse the flames. It took me forever to clean up the mess. For a long time after that I didn't venture back into the kitchen."

He plopped the two beefsteaks into the skillet, and the meat quickly seared and sizzled. After he'd arranged them just the way he wanted, he shot her a cheeky grin. "Stick with me, honey, and you'll never have to cook."

Not about to take the implication of his words seriously, she reached over and plucked a piece of lettuce from the head lying on the cabinet counter. She chewed thoughtfully before she finally asked, "Is your mother a kitchen person?"

He looked at her as though she might as well have asked if the woman was from Mars or some other far-off planet. "You've got to be joking. Mom wouldn't know a spatula from a meat cleaver."

From the impression Ridge had given her of his life at home, she'd not expected his mother to be the homey sort. Still, she'd asked in hopes that Mrs. Garroway had sometimes had motherly moments.

"So she wasn't one of those mothers who baked cookies for school functions or made popcorn balls to eat in front of the television."

"Hardly," he said with a grimace. "Mom doesn't watch television. She thinks it's beneath her. She'd rather sit around with a cocktail and whine about how lonely and bored she is."

Nicolette watched his features tighten and she suddenly realized she wanted to know everything about this man. His hopes and dreams, and even his disappointments, had become important to her. "You don't get along with your parents at all, do you?"

He turned away from the skillet of sizzling steaks to face her. "Frankly, no. We have nothing in common. I'm sorry, too. Because it's not the way I'd like for things to be."

"Have you tried to compromise with

them?" she asked carefully. "From what you told me before, I can understand you don't like their lifestyle. But maybe if you give in just a little—"

His cynical snort stopped just short of being angry. "There is no compromising or sharing with the Garroways, Nicci. It's their way or no way." He turned back to the skillet and shoved a fork at the cooking meat. "I had a phone call from my mother this evening before you came down to my office," he went on, his voice softening a bit. "She called to remind me that I was embarrassing my father by living in a shack and working for practically nothing. To hear her tell it, he won't be able to hold his head up until I go home to Houston. I keep telling her that my home is here now, but she won't listen. And Dad, well, he pretty much disowned me a long time ago."

Her heart aching for him, she stepped closer. "Why?"

She watched his features tighten.

"Because I didn't follow in the traditional Garroway footsteps. According to him, I'm a good-for-nothing rebel."

Unable to understand such narrow mindedness, Nicolette shook her head with amazement. "You became a doctor like him. Which took years of diligent work and study. Wasn't that enough?"

"Not at all. The Garroways have an image to uphold. Or so they think. I ruined things by moving away, by defying the long-standing years of Richard Garroway being a noted neurosurgeon in Houston."

Her gaze traveled to his strong, tanned hands. One was gripping the handle of the iron skillet. The other was holding a long-handled fork. Both looked like a working-man's hands instead of those of a pampered surgeon. Memory told her that the palms were slightly callused and just rough enough to cause a pleasant friction as they smoothed across her skin. She tried not to shiver at the erotic thought.

She said, "From what I've been told, you do perform some surgeries."

He nodded. "Minor things. Like pacemakers. Anything else that involves opening the heart, I refer."

"Did you choose not to do those major surgeries to defy your father? Or was there some other reason?"

Faint annoyance arched his brow as he glanced at her. "Nicci, you've been misreading me. I'm not defying anyone. I'm simply living my life the way I want to live it. Instead of the way someone else wants me to. I'm not just a doctor. I'm a cowboy, too. I like both professions, and while I'm out working on a fence or with horses, or anything else for that matter, I don't want to have to worry about squashing or cutting a finger. Besides all that, I don't want to be tied down to a grueling schedule. I want time for a wife and children. Real time. Not just a few minutes here and there." He turned away from the gas range to face her. "Does that disappoint you?"

The question struck Nicolette so hard that she had to glance away from his probing gaze. When her marriage to Bill had started to falter, she'd thrown herself into her work. She'd devoted every minute of her days and most of her nights to her patients. She'd convinced herself that the only good doctor was a devoted one, one who cared for his patients first and his own family second. After all, she'd tried putting Bill foremost in her life and she'd gotten nothing but heartache in return. At least her patients had appreciated her.

Yet Ridge was telling her that he wanted his family to be the most important thing to him. Meeting a man like him at this point in her life was almost bittersweet.

"Of course it doesn't disappoint me," she said huskily, even though her heart wasn't in the words. She was a bit disappointed but not for the reason he thought. She was saddened because she knew she couldn't be his *special* woman. The one who would eventually make a life with him here in this cozy ranch house or the one that would give him children. "Why should it?"

Faint humor twisted his lips. "Because you think a doctor is supposed to turn his life over to his patients."

Turning her head back to him, Nicolette looked at him crossly. "I never said that."

"You didn't have to. I can read between your words."

He was mixing her up, turning her thinking in one direction and then another. She let out a hefty sigh of frustration. "Look, Ridge, I tried mixing a medical career and a marriage. It didn't work out for me."

"So you think I can't make it work, either?"

Shaking her head, she tried to quell the strange emotions swirling around inside her. A part of her wanted him to have everything he wanted, especially happiness. But when she thought of him with a wife and children, she couldn't stop the selfish longing eating at her insides.

"I didn't say that," she answered finally. "I just think…it would be a very hard balancing act. Unless you found the right woman."

A slow smile spread across his face and crinkled the corners of his brown eyes. "She's out there, Nicci. And I plan to find her."

Nicci's heart fluttered like a hummingbird's wing as she waited for him to go on with some flirtatious line—that he was looking at the right woman. Or that he'd already found the perfect woman and she was standing right next to him. But he didn't say any of those things. Nicolette hated herself for letting the whole idea leave her feeling as flat as a pancake. What did she expect? She'd taken herself off the market for love and marriage.

"Good luck," she murmured, then turned toward the head of lettuce draining on a paper towel. "I'll make a salad while the meat finishes cooking. Do you want tomato?"

She'd hardly gotten the question out when his arms came around her from behind and his lips nuzzled the side of her neck.

"You're what I want, Nicci," he mouthed against her ear. "Hell, you knew that when you agreed to come here tonight."

She swallowed as a thousand butterfly wings rose up in her stomach and attempted to fly out of her throat. "Maybe I did," she murmured. "And maybe I knew that coming here wasn't a wise thing for me to do."

His arms tightened around her waist. "Then why did you?"

Shrugging helplessly, she turned and lifted her face up to his. "Because I like being with you," she answered honestly. "Because you make me feel…special."

Surprise flickered across his face. Then his head bent and he pressed his cheek against hers. "Oh, honey, honey," he whispered, "you make me feel more than special—you turn me inside out. Ever since last weekend I've wanted to get you back into my arms. You're the only thing I can think about—all I want to think about."

His declaration left her breathless and unable to utter a word. But after his lips fastened roughly over hers it didn't matter that she'd failed to make any sort of reply.

Kissing Ridge again was pure excitement backed with sweet joy. As his lips searched and plundered, her senses spun faster and faster until her hands were clenching the front of his shirt for stability.

When he finally lifted his head long enough for her to breathe, she warned in a raw voice, "The steaks are going to burn."

With a seductive chuckle, he said, "Too late. I've already put them on a platter."

His hands were moving in slow, sensual circles against her back, and she felt a coil of longing wrap itself around her loins. "Then we should be eating them," she whispered frantically.

Lower and lower his hands dipped until his fingers were cupping the curve of her bottom. "The steaks can be reheated."

"You can be, too," she pointed out.

Another chuckle slipped past his lips. "See what I like about you being older than me? You're confident."

"No! I'm not!" she spluttered. "Right now I'm scared to death."

Grabbing for a cool breath of sanity, she ducked under his arm and crossed to the opposite side of the kitchen. But before she had time to glance over her shoulder, Ridge had already followed and was standing just as close as he'd been before.

Touching a forefinger beneath her chin, he asked gently, "Why are you scared, Nicci?"

Her heart was pounding like the hooves on a runaway horse, and the crazy thought ran through her head that she was going to end up needing him as a doctor even more than she wanted him as a man.

"Because we can't...shouldn't be doing this."

Flattening his hand, he cupped the palm against the side of her face. Like a cat seeking its master's hand, Nicolette closed her eyes and cherished the feeling of his skin against hers.

"Doing what?" he asked softly. "Making love?"

Heat consumed her face. "Yes."

His hand slipped to the back of her head and unfastened the barrette holding her hair. Instantly the heavy weight of brown tresses fell against her back and around her shoulders. Nicolette could hardly breathe as he thrust his fingers into the waves and combed them back from her face.

"I want you and you want me. What else really matters?" he asked.

What else? There were plenty of things that should matter. That would eventually matter. But at the moment she couldn't think of a one. Not when a deep, unbidden hunger for him was spiraling through her, making it impossible to resist all that he was offering.

"Nothing, Ridge. Nothing at all."

Chapter Nine

The half-prepared meal was instantly forgotten as Ridge enveloped Nicolette in a tight embrace and sealed her lips with a long, simmering kiss.

As the heat of his body spread into hers, she abandoned the last niggling reservations in her mind and quickly slipped her arms up and around his neck. The silent response caused his kiss to deepen until the urgency to get closer turned into an intangible need for both of them.

Easing his lips from hers, he whispered, "Let's go to the bedroom."

By then Nicolette's senses were so drugged with desire for him that all she could manage was a slight nod. The signal was all he needed, and he quickly slipped his hand around hers and led her out of the kitchen.

His was a small room with a bed of dark oak pushed into one corner, a matching dresser at the opposite end, and a tall chest of the same wood positioned a few steps from the head of the bed.

The floor was oiled parquet with a huge braided rug at the bedside. The unbleached muslin curtains were closed, shutting out the lingering twilight of the evening.

For a brief moment, as her gaze skittered around his intimate sleeping place, Nicolette asked herself if she'd gone crazy. It wasn't like her to behave in such a reckless, impulsive way. But then, she'd never felt so aroused, so full of need for any man. She couldn't hide or run from her feelings now. Her throbbing body wouldn't let her.

Ridge brought them to a stop on the braided rug, but he didn't immediately lay her on the bed. Instead, both his hands carefully cupped her face and then he bent his warm mouth back down to hers.

As his kiss heated her blood, his fingers

went to work with the belt around her waist. Once he had it unbuckled, he allowed the wide piece of leather to fall away. The belt hardly had time to hit the floor when he reached for the buttons on her white shirt.

His fingers dispensed with the tiny fasteners one by one, while the brush of his hands against her breasts sent shocks of hot pleasure dancing along her veins. As soon as he peeled the white cotton from her shoulders, his head bent, and she groaned out loud when his mouth planted itself in the hollow between her small breasts.

He kissed her there, then licked and nibbled his way across the flesh spilling over the lacy cups of her bra. While his tongue danced over her skin, his fingers reached between her shoulder blades and unfastened the scrap of lace covering her breasts.

Nicolette stood motionless, her heart beating in her throat as he pulled the shirttails from the waist of her skirt, then pushed both garments off her shoulders to send them tumbling to the floor at their feet.

She watched those brown eyes of his fasten on her pert breasts and was amazed to see him smile as though he'd uncovered a precious treasure.

"Beautiful."

His one murmured word was enough to send a warm, embarrassed flush over her entire body. "I'm not twenty anymore," she countered in a strained voice.

His smile deepened. "Neither am I."

His quirky reply very nearly made her laugh. But the sound died in her throat as he suddenly dipped his mouth to one hard, chocolate-colored nipple. As he rolled the sensitive bud between his teeth and tongue, her head fell back, while a moan sounded in her throat.

Desperate to hold on, to keep him close, she thrust her hands in his hair. Moist, aching heat burned between her thighs, shocking her, thrilling her with the ultimate pleasure of being a woman.

She didn't know how long his mouth made a lazy foray of her breasts. Time had ceased since they'd entered the room and she was only aware of feeling the cool quilt beneath her back.

Brown high heels teetered on her toes, then fell to the braided rug with a muffled thump, thump.

Ridge placed one last kiss on her mouth, then stood to remove his own clothing.

While he dealt with his slacks and shirt, she wiggled out of her skirt and draped it over the footboard.

Once he was standing naked, gazing down at her he said in a low, husky voice, "I hope you're protected because I don't want to have to use a condom. I want to feel every inch of you against me."

She'd not been expecting him to say anything so erotic. She was embarrassed and aroused at the same time. Thankfully the room had grown dim enough to hide the blush on her face.

"I'm on the Pill," she said lowly. "For regularity reasons."

Smiling wickedly now, he joined her on the bed and pulled her into his arms. Nicolette sighed with abandon and turned her face to search for his lips.

He rewarded her with a kiss so consuming all she could do was grip his shoulders and try to match the wild, slanting search of his lips, the hungry thrust of his tongue.

Like dust picked up by a slow-moving whirlwind, her senses spun round and round, up and up into a tight funnel of aching need. She'd never felt so out of control, so desperate to be possessed.

His hands were everywhere; his fingers warm bands exploring her back, trekking across her belly, gliding over her breasts. Between his thumb and forefinger, her nipples tightened with pleasure and anticipation. His mouth eased against hers and he nibbled and chewed at her lower lip.

Raw passion was digging, building deep within her, slicking her body with sweat and shortening her breath to quick, silent sups of air.

"Ridge—" She gasped his name while her head twisted from one side to the other. "This is—I want you. Really want you!"

He smiled against her mouth. "Good. That's the way it's supposed to be."

Against her thighs she could feel the soft abrasion of his hairy legs, the brush of his rigid manhood. The idea that she'd lifted him to such a state of arousal was as intoxicating as a swift shot of whiskey. She'd never thought of herself as sexy, but Ridge was definitely making her feel that way.

Lifting his head away from hers, he looked down at her body. Night shadows were drifting into the room, mottling her skin, painting the dips and valleys with soft gray. He trailed his knuckles down the crease of her midriff.

"I knew you would look this way," he said thickly. "Soft, smooth curves just waiting to be touched. You feel like a piece of satin, my darling Nicci."

Bending his head, he brushed his lips along the trail his knuckles had taken. Nicolette's eyelids fluttered down, her teeth bit into her lower lip as pleasure invaded every cell of her body. A sigh whispered past her lips then turned into a needy groan as his mouth dipped lower and lower.

Gripping his shoulders, she waited for the exploration to stop and the coupling of their bodies to begin. She had to feel him inside her, possessing her. Otherwise her body was going to go up in flames.

"And you make me feel—glorious—too glorious. Oh, my. Oh Ridge—" she choked. "Make love to me."

Her plea sent his fingers to the juncture of her thighs. He touched the moist folds, teased them with the gentle brush of his fingertips until Nicolette was writhing with need.

She was arching against him, her body straining for release when he finally dipped his head even lower and separated the folds of her womanhood with his tongue.

The totally erotic contact was more than Nicolette could bear. He'd barely had the chance to taste her when bright stars exploded behind her eyes and she cried out his name.

When her senses finally drifted back to earth, her eyes were misty, her body limp. "Ridge—you—I didn't know. Until now. Until you."

The wondrous look in her gray eyes not only surprised him, it swelled his chest with an emotion too big to understand. His throat was thick when he tried to speak. "Darling, Nicci. I want to please you. That's what makes me happy—very happy."

Her eyes were full of tenderness as they slipped over his face and then, with a helpless groan, she pulled him down to her.

Ridge felt his body spiraling out of control as her soft hands skimmed his back, his shoulders and chest, then caught his hips and guided them to hers. He'd wanted to wait before he joined his body to hers. He'd wanted to prolong the exquisite moments of touching her, of watching the rich expressions of desire cross her beautiful face. But the fierce need to have her warmth surrounding him, caressing him, was even greater.

Somehow he managed to enter her slowly, but by the time she began to move against him his head was reeling, his loins on fire. Her legs wrapped around his as their bodies rocked to a rapid, hungry rhythm. Sweat covered him as he fought to stay afloat, to hold back the rush of need building inside him.

Her soft whimpers eventually turned into urgent cries and when she raised her head to search for his mouth, he fastened his lips over hers and let his warm seed spill into her.

Ridge didn't know how long it took his wilted body to collect enough strength to roll away from her. For the first time in his life, he'd lost all sense of time and place. Making love to Nicolette had sent him somewhere else, and the journey back had left him shocked and disoriented.

The cool air separating their bodies had him reaching for her again. He groaned with utter contentment as she rolled against his side and rested her head on his shoulder.

"That was beautiful," he murmured, yet even as he said the words he realized they were too trite to describe what had just taken place between them. Beautiful, glorious, mind-bending. None of those came close to the euphoria he'd felt.

His chest was still rising and falling at a fairly rapid rate. Nicolette's small hand lay against the beating of his heart, until he lifted it to his lips and kissed each slender finger.

"I'm so embarrassed," she whispered.

Her remark had him tilting his head so he could see her face. "Why?"

"Because—" Her head stirred and she brought her eyes up to his. "I thought I knew what being with a man was all about. But you've shown me that I didn't know...it wasn't like this before, Ridge."

The confusion and honesty he heard in her voice pierced him in a way that was both sweet and painful. He stroked her damp hair. "I guess I should be telling you that I'm sorry your sex life was lacking. But I'm too selfish a man for that. I'm glad it was better with me, Nicci."

Nicolette was also glad, yet there was another part of her that was terrified. No man had ever made her lose control as Ridge just had. She'd always been a methodical woman, one who tried to keep careful control over her emotions. But he'd just stripped away all of that, and she was afraid of the reckless, needy woman he was exposing.

"I didn't plan on this happening between us tonight," she confessed.

"I honestly wasn't planning on it, either," he admitted, then added with a wicked chuckle, "but I'm damn glad it did."

Rolling toward her, he placed a hand on her shoulder, then slid it to her bare hip. The simple touch was enough to stir her remnants of desire and push away the doubts she knew would come later.

"So am I," she whispered, then brought her lips against his. "Are you ready for supper?"

With a pleased chuckle, he rolled onto his back and pulled her along so that she was sprawled over the top of him. "Forget about supper. We'll cook some eggs and add it to the steaks for breakfast."

The next morning Nicolette was sitting at the long pine table in the Saddler kitchen as she absently slathered peach jam onto half of a buttermilk biscuit. Across the way, Cook eyed the bird-size portions on Nicolette's plate and scolded her soundly.

"You're gonna wind up having to doctor yourself, Miss Nicci, if you keep up that sort of eating. I've never seen such silliness in you young women today. Trying to starve yourself down to bones. Now just look at me." Not bothering to put down the dish-towel or stewing pot she'd been drying, she held out both arms. "I ain't fat and I ate three times the breakfast that's on your plate."

"I'm not sick, Cook. I'm just not hungry," Nicolette told her. How could she be, she thought wryly. It had only been a few short hours since she and Ridge had finally gotten around to eating the steaks he'd cooked. She was still full from the meal, not to mention groggy from lack of sleep.

Ridge had tried his best to persuade her to spend the night with him, but Nicolette had refused to take things that far. In the first place, her mother had known she was going to have dinner with Ridge. If she hadn't come home to the ranch last night, her mother would have easily put two and two together, and Nicci wasn't ready to deal with Geral-dine's suppositions. Secondly, she'd not wanted to give Ridge the impression that she was handing her life over to him. Because she wasn't. She couldn't. Being his lover was one thing, but being anything more was out of the question. He was too young. And she was too warped to ever be the wife he wanted and needed.

Forcing her attention back to Cook, she

said, "You're naturally slim and beautiful. Some of us just have to work harder than you do. Now quit scolding me. I'll have a big lunch later today. I promise."

"Flattery like that don't cut any ice with me, missy," she said with a snort before she turned back to her task at the kitchen counter.

"Good morning, ladies! Glorious morning, isn't it?"

Both Nicolette and Cook turned at the sound of Geraldine's cheerful voice to see the matriarch of the Sandbur ranch saunter into the kitchen.

She was dressed in slim blue jeans and a starched yellow shirt with a brown bandanna tied at her neck. Coral and silver earrings dangled from her ears, and her silver hair was brushed into a sleek style that swished against her shoulders. Any signs of the bronchitis that had nearly hospitalized her a few weeks ago were now totally gone.

"Well, don't you look spiffy this morning," Cook commented as the other woman filled a plate from bowls of food laid out on a buffet table.

"Are you going somewhere, Mother?" Nicolette asked curiously as she watched her mother push the plate of food into a microwave.

Geraldine's smile was faint and just a bit secretive. "I am. Wolfe is taking me to the horse sale up at Seguin today."

Nicolette's mouth popped open. "The horse sale! Cordero says we need to be selling horses not buying more of them." Then her eyes narrowed with interest as the other part of her mother's comment connected with her brain. "Wolfe. You mean Wolfe Maddson? The state senator here in Goliad County?"

"That's right. You met him at Matt and Juliet's wedding. Tall, good-looking man."

Geraldine took a seat at the table and began to eat. Nicolette exchanged a curious glance with Cook before she turned to her mother.

"Uh, I thought the senator was married."

"His wife passed away last year from a lingering disease. I've been urging him to get out and do something—other than his work up at the Capital."

"Hmm, well it sounds like he's finally taking your advice. I hope you two enjoy the day," Nicolette said and meant it. Even though she really didn't know Senator Maddson all that well, she trusted her mother to use common sense in matters of men. After all, Geraldine had chosen a wonderful mate and father to her children. She'd had the good judgment to marry a man capable of loving her deeply, who had stood by her side until his untimely death. Whereas Nicolette had allowed her heart to be carried off by a man who'd been as shallow as the San Antonio River in the middle of a drought. No. She didn't have to worry about her mother. Geraldine Saddler knew her way around a man. It was her own heart that Nicolette needed to worry about. And after last night she was beginning to wonder if she'd left it with Ridge.

"What about you, honey? How did your supper with Ridge go last night?" Geraldine asked.

Nicolette started to drop the last bite of biscuit onto her plate but, fearing Cook was watching, she tossed it into her mouth and dutifully chewed.

"It was fine. Nice," she eventually replied.

Picking up her coffee cup, Geraldine tossed her daughter a faintly annoyed look. "That's all? Nice?"

Nicolette shrugged. "Well, what do you want me to say?"

"I was hoping I'd come in here and find roses on your cheeks." Reaching over, she caught Nicolette by the chin and angled her face one way and then the other. "Instead, you look pale and drained."

Pink color swathed Nicolette's cheeks, but thankfully it came after her mother had removed her hand and turned her attention back to eating.

"I look drained because I had a long day yesterday and I stayed later at Ridge's than I'd intended." At least that much was true, she thought. Much later. The clock had been close to striking two when she'd finally crawled into her own bed this morning. It was indecent. But for the first time in her life she felt sexy and wanted.

"What was his home like?" Geraldine persisted.

Nicolette smiled as she scooted forward on her chair. At least this was something she could share with her mother.

"I actually loved it. It's small and homey and has two long porches with all sorts of furniture and potted plants. A huge pecan tree shades the yard and there's an old chicken house in the back that Ridge is going to restore. He's even going to get some laying hens. I told him to get dominickers. They lay the best. Isn't that right, Cook?"

"That's right," Cook answered from her place at the counter. "But what's he gonna do about coyotes? Does he know it'll take one coyote about two nights to clear out a chicken house?"

"He has a German shepherd dog named Enoch," Nicolette answered. "I'm sure he'll keep the coyotes chased away."

"Then he really is going to make this area his home," Geraldine mused aloud.

A faint frown creased Nicolette's forehead. "That's been his intention from the start. But he—well, he can't convince his parents, especially his mother of that. She's badgering him to return to Houston. And his father will hardly speak to Ridge because he's here rather than there." Her voice softened as regret for him filled her heart. "Oh, Mother, he doesn't say that the estrangement hurts him, but I can tell that it does. I wish his parents would understand what a fine young man he is instead of trying to bend him to their will."

Geraldine glanced up and, after taking a moment to scan Nicolette's troubled face, laid a gentle hand over her daughter's. "It sounds as though you're beginning to care for Dr. Garroway."

Did she? After last night she felt foolish to even ask herself that question. From the first night she'd rushed to the hospital and found him treating Dan in such a personal way, she'd cared about him. But now that initial caring seemed to be growing, blossoming into something that made her feel like the world around her was bright and beautiful. She didn't want to fall in love. That wasn't in her plans. But her heart didn't seem to be following her instructions.

Breathing deeply, she wiped her fingers on a napkin and then reached for her coffee. "I do care for him, Mother. But I—don't want things to get too serious between us. He's a man I enjoy being with, and that's where it stops."

"Why?" Geraldine persisted. "And don't start in about Bill and all that bull he put you through. Ridge isn't Bill. He's far from it."

"That's sure saying a mouthful," Cook spoke up, her voice full of grit. "I'd still like to take Bill out somewhere and scare the hell out of him with my shotgun."

Ignoring Hattie's comment, Nicolette said to her mother, "I'm nine years older than Ridge, Mom. That's eventually bound to cause problems."

"Not if you don't let it."

So Ridge had said, too, Nicolette thought wearily. She might as well forget that argument for the time being. "Okay, put that reason out of your mind and think about this. Ridge is a busy doctor and so am I. We'd never have time for much of a life together. He deserves more than that. He—" She paused as her throat thickened with emotion, and before Geraldine could spot the glaze of tears in her eyes, she turned her gaze to the windows looking out over the back patio and the garden beyond. She swallowed before she finally spoke. "Ridge wants a wife and children."

"Well, hallelujah. At last. You've found a man who wants the same things as you," Geraldine exclaimed. "I think that's wonderful."

Dismally, Nicolette turned back to her mother. "I thought Bill wanted the same things I did. Look what that got me. No, Mom, I'm not ready to put my trust in a man again. I just can't do it."

Scooting back her chair, she rose from the table to leave the kitchen. Her mother swiftly caught her by the forearm.

"Honey, you just agreed that Ridge is nothing like your ex-husband. So why can't you trust him?"

Why couldn't she, Nicolette asked herself.

How could she explain that to her mother when she couldn't even explain it to herself?

"It doesn't matter, Mother. Ridge is hardly proposing marriage." And if he did, she'd have to tell him no. Everything between them would have to end. It was something she couldn't bear to think about.

Across the room Cook said, "Men are just like horses, Miss Nicci. Some are outlaws and others you can trust with your life. Cordero says a good horse can't be picked by its conformation or whether it has high-toned breeding. It's that soft look in the horse's eye that tells him he's a keeper." She glanced over her shoulder at Nicolette. "I liked Ridge right off. Not because he's mighty good to look at. He has that soft eye. And I'm thinkin' he has it for you."

Chapter Ten

While Nicolette was making an awkward exit from the Saddler kitchen, Ridge was sitting at his office desk, staring absently at the window instead of the insurance papers lying on his desk.

His lawyer had sent a series of documents for him to sign regarding the malpractice insurance he needed, to protect his medical profession from lawsuit-happy lawyers. Ridge had read them over and had found the cost of the policy to be worse than criminal. He'd wanted to tear the papers into tiny bits. He'd wanted to call the most influential politician he could think of and blast him or her with the problems of rising medical costs and the reasons why. But Ridge had never been a man to hold on to his anger for more than a few short minutes. It was a wasteful emotion. Besides that, he couldn't think about anything except the woman he'd made love to last night.

With a plaintive sigh, he rose from the desk and walked over to the windows overlooking the parking lot. It had only been a few short hours since he'd driven Nicolette back here to the clinic to pick up her car. He'd practically begged her to stay the remainder of the night with him. He'd wanted to feel her sleeping beside him. He'd wanted to wake and see her head pillowed on his shoulder. He'd wanted her to make that small but first step of commitment. But she'd refused with all sorts of arguments. None of which had been the real crux of her reason to bolt. He could see it plainly. She was afraid of giving in to him and to herself.

But was her fear coming solely from her bad marriage? Or was he falling for another Brittany? Was Nicolette really running from his modest lifestyle and his break from a wealthy inheritance?

No. Ridge didn't want to think about that just yet. The fact that she'd made love to him had to be enough for now.

Enough. That thought elicited a silent groan within him. The things she'd made him feel last night far exceeded enough. She'd stolen his breath, his very heart and soul. He couldn't envision his life without her.

He was still in deep contemplation, telling himself he had to get ready for his first patient of the day, when the telephone on his desk rang. Before he picked it up he could see the call was coming from his receptionist's desk.

"Yes, Saundra."

"I'm sorry to disturb you, Dr. Garroway, but Saddler is calling from her office. She says it's important that she talk with you. She's on line three. Do you want to take the call or shall I tell her to call back later?"

Ridge shoved back his cuff to see he had fifteen minutes before his first appointment. "No. I'll take the call. Thank you, Saundra."

Quickly he punched the buttons that would connect him to Nicolette's call.

"Hello, Nicci."

"Good morning, Ridge. Sorry to bother you so early. I know you're getting ready to see patients, but I need to meet with you for a few minutes if I could."

His brows lifted with surprise while his voice lowered. "Is this about last night?"

A slight pause crossed the line and then she said in a husky tone, "No. But I have been thinking about last night—about you—and all of it has been fairly naughty."

His body stirred with desire and he drew in a deep breath and quickly pushed it out. "Same here."

She suddenly cleared her throat. "I have a little patient here I want you to take a look at. But if you don't have the time, I'll have my receptionist make an appointment for him with you."

"I have the time. I'll be right down."

He quickly cut the connection, then called his receptionist to tell her he'd be out for a few minutes. Once he'd hung up the phone, he exited the suite of his office suite through a back hallway and hurried across the building to Nicolette's office.

The moment he stepped into the waiting room a nurse with a thick head of bright-red curls ushered him back to an examining room at the back of the hallway.

Nicolette was inside, along with a thin,

young woman who hardly appeared to be out of her teens. A small baby of about three or four months of age was lying on his back in the middle of the examining table. The infant's thin arms were flailing in the air while his intermittent cries of frustration were causing the young woman to smooth her fingers over the top of his head.

Ridge sensed a thread of urgency as Nicolette quickly introduced him to the mother. "Dr. Garroway, this is Meghan Delaney. She's David's mother."

He shook the woman's hand. "Nice to meet you, Ms. Delaney. Are you having a problem with David?"

Meghan Delaney gave him an anxious nod. "He cries all the time and he's not gaining weight like he should. I try to feed him more, but he just doesn't want his bottle or cereal."

Ridge glanced questioningly at Nicolette who was standing at the head of the examining table. "Do you act as his pediatrician?"

Nicolette gave him a negative shake of her head. "No. Ms. Delaney gave birth to David at home with the help of a midwife. The baby has never seen a doctor until this morning."

"I see," Ridge said. But frankly he didn't. Sometimes it amazed him to hear the reasons some people used to avoid doctors and medical facilities. In Ms. Delaney's case he figured it was money and misguidance from someone close to her. Her clothes were frayed and wrinkled, her thin brown hair pulled into a ponytail. He didn't see a wedding ring on her finger and he very much doubted she was married. But it was the dull, lifeless look in her eyes that told of her plight. Ridge wanted only to comfort and reassure her that her world would eventually get better.

"Have you started a chart on him?" he asked Nicolette.

She gestured to the red-headed nurse who was standing in the far corner of the small room. "Jacki, show Dr. Garroway the vital stats you've recorded," she instructed.

The nurse stepped forward and handed Ridge a manila folder with one lone slip of paper inside. He read it over quickly then turned back to the child. The baby had dark eyes, sparse, reddish-brown hair and a complexion that was too pale to be healthy. Yet he had a sweet, cherub face that couldn't help but make Ridge smile.

"Okay, little guy, let's see what's going on here."

Before he'd left his office, Ridge had stuffed a stethoscope into the pocket of his lab coat. Now he fastened the instrument around his neck and began to warm the round metal end with his hand.

"Dr. Saddler says you mend hearts," the young girl spoke to Ridge in a worried voice. "Does that mean my little Davey has something wrong with his heart? Is that why she wants you to look at him?"

Ridge smiled gently at her. "Well, let me listen to him first and then we'll talk about it," he answered carefully as he bent over the baby.

Sensing that a stranger was drawing near, David began to cry in earnest, making it impossible for Ridge to hear what was going on inside the baby's chest.

Nicolette was about to gesture for Jacki to pick up the baby and try to quiet him, when Ridge reached down and lifted the tiny boy into his arms.

"Here, now, little fellow," he crooned to the baby, "I'm not going to hurt you. I'm going to make you feel better. And then you'll be too busy growing and playing to cry."

He rocked the child for a moment and the cries quieted. Finally the three women watched in amazement as Ridge pulled a cell phone from his trouser pocket and handed it to baby. "Here," he said. "Chew on this."

As if he understood every word Ridge had said to him, David wrapped his tiny fingers around the folded plastic and took it straight to his mouth. After that Ridge had no problem laying the baby down on the table and listening to his chest and back.

Once he was finished, he cradled the baby back in his arms and looked at the mother.

"It sounds as though David has a heart murmur. That's why he's not gaining weight and crying most of the time. He feels tired because his heart isn't working right."

The young woman visibly wilted, and Nicolette quickly put a supportive arm around her shoulders. "Don't panic, Meghan," she softly encouraged. "Dr. Garroway will take good care of your son."

Meghan turned worried, but hopeful eyes on Ridge. "What is a murmur? Can you make him well?"

Ridge glanced down at the baby cradled in the crook of his left arm and wondered what it would feel like to hold his own son. Instinctively his gaze lifted to Nicolette and as she caught the beam of his eyes with hers, the heat of their lovemaking came roaring to the forefront of his mind. If not for her birth control, she could be pregnant with his child right now. It was a soaring thought.

But he wasn't here to think about loving Nicolette or having a child with her. At the moment, his first priority was little David.

To answer Meghan's question, he said, " A murmur is a sound that happens when a valve in the heart isn't working right. Valves have lids and when those lids don't close or open properly blood leaks out or can't get through to the place it needs to go."

The woman looked even more horrified. "That sounds awful! What can you do? Will he ever get well?"

With each question her voice rose to a higher, more frantic pitch. Nicolette patted her shoulder. "It's okay, Meghan. Don't get scared. I promised you that Dr. Garroway would take care of David. Your son will grow to be a strong young man. That's what we all want."

Ridge handed the baby over to his mother. "David will need to have some extensive tests done. Some of them I can do here in the clinic. Others may have to be done in the hospital. Once I get the results, then we can decide what he needs to make him well. Okay?"

The baby's mother stared at him in a shell-shocked way. "Doctor, I don't have insurance or much money. That's why I brought David to see Dr. Saddler. Someone told me she saw patients for free. I can't pay for all those things to be done for my baby."

Money. It wasn't right that a human life had to depend on it for survival. As far as Ridge was concerned, having the stuff was more of an albatross than anything else. But then he'd never been like Meghan Delaney. Neither had Nicolette. And he wondered if either of them could really understand what it would be like to be in the poor woman's shoes.

Smiling gently at her, he shook his head. "Don't worry about the expense. We'll make sure that everything is taken care of and that David gets the care he needs."

He twisted his head around in search of the redheaded nurse and noticed for the first time the name pin on her uniform. Jacki. Apparently she was the nurse who'd talked Nicolette into having dinner with him last night. He needed to remember to thank the woman.

"Jacki, would you show Ms. Delaney and her son down to my office and tell the receptionist to make space for David this morning."

"Of course, Dr. Garroway," Jacki told him, then with a kindly smile ushered the woman and child toward the door.

As the three of them were about to exit the small examining room, Jacki realized the baby was still chewing happily on Ridge's cell phone. "Oh here, you're going to need your phone back, Dr. Garroway."

"Let him have it for a toy," Ridge spoke up. "I have another in my office. I'll just activate it."

Meghan Delaney looked over her shoulder, her gaze encompassing both Ridge and Nicolette. "Thank you," she said in a strained but grateful voice. "Thank you both."

Jacki shut the door firmly behind them and Ridge turned to Nicolette. "So Dr. Saddler sees patients for free." He clucked his tongue in teasing disapproval. "How do you expect the rest of us to compete with that?"

Shrugging, she gave him a sheepish smile. "I'm not here for the money. And apparently you aren't, either. Since when did doctors go around giving his cell phones to patients as toys? You know that woman can use up all your minutes."

"I hope she does." His expression sobered as he closed the short distance between them. "I'm glad you called me down here, Nicci. The baby needs attention."

"The moment I examined him, I knew he needed you." She looked at him earnestly. "Will he get well? I suppose I should have asked that question before I reassured the mother. But I happen to have unbounded faith in you."

The corners of his mouth curved ever so slightly upward as dimples came and went in his cheeks. "Really?"

Seeing the sudden gleam in his eye, she began to stutter, "Uh, as a doctor—that's what I'm talking about."

"Little David is going to be fine." Moving even closer, he placed his hands on either side of her waist and rested his forehead against hers. "What about you having faith in me as a man?" he murmured.

Being this close to him in a private place was one thing, but here in the clinic where anyone might walk in was something else. Yet she couldn't even glance at the door to make sure they were still alone, her gaze was too enthralled with his rugged face. So much for her resistance, she thought wryly.

"I do."

"You left this morning and I wanted you to stay."

Heat filled her cheeks as her heart thudded with excitement. "Just because I left doesn't mean I didn't want to stay," she admitted.

"Oh, Nicci, Nicci," he said with a groan. "Do you know what you do to me? How much I want you?"

He didn't give her time to answer. Instead his lips gathered hers up in a hot frantic union that brought Nicolette's blood to an immediate boil.

Even knowing that they could be interrupted at any moment wasn't enough to quell her desire for him. Her hands clung to his shoulders while her knees turned to mush. She'd just made love to the man only hours before, yet she wanted him again with a force that stunned her.

Both of them were breathing hard when he finally lifted his mouth away from hers and whispered, "I've got to be with you again, Nicci. Will you come to the house tonight?"

"I…I suppose. But Ridge, we can't go on like this." She attempted a protest, but she sounded lame, even to her own ears. Already her thoughts had leaped forward to the moment they could be together again.

"Why can't we?" he asked with a wicked grin, then, pulling away from her, he sauntered out the door before she could collect herself enough to answer.

Later that evening, Nicolette was sitting at her desk, attempting to finish the last of a pile of paper work when her private cell phone rang.

Expecting it to be her mother or someone from the ranch, she was more than surprised when Ridge's voice sounded in her ear. Since she'd only given him the number this morning, she hadn't expected him to use it so soon.

"Ridge. What are you doing? Are you already home?"

He sighed. "No. I'm at the hospital. I'm in an emergency situation with a patient, and there's no way of telling how soon I'll be finished," he answered.

Her spirits plummeted, even though common sense told her that she needed to cool things between them. "So, there's no need for me to come by your place tonight?"

"I'm sorry, Nicci. I don't want you to have to sit and wait for what could turn out to be hours. The patient is critical right now and I don't want to be too far away. I hope you understand."

Of course she understood, but that didn't make her feel any better. All day she'd dreamed about seeing him again. Her heart had been planning on it. Now she had to go home and deal with her own lonely company, something she'd been doing for years but which tonight seemed unappealing.

"I do, Ridge. I wouldn't want you to leave the patient—especially not for me. We, uh, we'll get together later."

His voice lowered. "I hate this, Nicci. I want to see you so badly. You know that, don't you?"

Her gaze fastened on the yellow roses on her desk. She'd take the bouquet home with her tonight and maybe they'd give her a measure of comfort. But nothing would take the place of having his arms around her. The realization frightened her. She couldn't let Ridge become the most important thing in her life. That would mean she loved him. And she couldn't let herself make that mistake again.

"Yes."

"We'll try again tomorrow night. Okay?"

Her sigh was so soft it was inaudible to his ears.

"All right, Ridge. If things are quiet after work tomorrow evening, I'll see you then."

"Great! I gotta go now. Bye, my sweet girl."

He quickly cut the connection and Nicolette slowly shut off her phone and tossed it into her purse.

Barely able to suppress her disappointment, she finished off the last of the paperwork. She was stuffing reports to read at home into her briefcase when Jacki entered the office.

"All done out here," she announced cheerfully. "Ready to lock up?"

Nodding, Nicolette jammed the briefcase under one arm, then reached for the roses with both hands.

"I'm ready. Would you hold the door open for me?" she asked.

"You're taking the roses home with you? Why? I thought you liked having them on your desk," Jacki reasoned.

"I do. But I…well, I just thought it would be nice to have them at home with me before they wilt."

"Speaking of wilting, you look like you've just lost your best friend," Jacki remarked with a thoughtful glance at her. "But since I'm still here, that can't be your problem. Has something happened at the ranch?"

"No." Nicolette started to give her friend a half-baked excuse for her mood, then decided at the last minute to tell the truth. "Actually, Jacki, I had plans again with Ridge tonight. But they just fell through. He has an emergency going on over at the hospital."

"Oh. I'm sorry." She looked at Nicolette with faint surprise. "I didn't realize you were planning on seeing him again this soon. Are things getting serious between you?"

Nicolette's gaze fell to the graceful yellow rosebuds gathered against her chest. For the past few days she'd felt like a young woman being courted, and maybe she'd let the excitement of being wooed by a handsome man like Ridge skew the reality of the situation. Maybe she wasn't nearly as important to him as he was becoming to her.

Sighing, Nicolette started walking toward the door. "I don't know how to answer that, Jacki. A part of me wants to get serious about Ridge. But then the practical part of me—" she paused and shrugged, while behind her, Jacki opened the door so that Nicolette could maneuver through the opening with the huge bouquet.

"Worries," Jacki finished for her. "Nicci, you'll never find true love if you don't let yourself look for it."

Groaning, Nicci stepped through the door

and waited in the hallway while Jacki made sure the lock was secured. "And make another huge mistake?" she asked bitterly.

Jacki gave her a pointed look. "Dear Nicci, mistakes aren't the end of things. They're just opportunities to learn."

Thirty minutes later, when Nicolette arrived home, she was still thinking about Jacki's sage remark. What had she learned from her mistakes with Bill? That all men were not to be trusted? That most of them should be slinking through the woods on their bellies? No. Her ruined marriage had taught her that she'd given her love to a man without really knowing him. True, Bill had deliberately lied, but she should have looked closer. She should have been perceptive enough to pick up on the clues of his dark side. Instead she'd been blinded by love.

Dear God, don't let Ridge blind me all over again, she prayed.

Later that evening she was sitting down to a solitary supper when her mother burst into the kitchen. Her face was full of excitement as she hurried over to where her daughter sat at the pine table.

"Nicci, just wait until you see what I got at the sale today! They're adorable! Hurry up and finish your plate. I want you to come down to the barn with me."

Geraldine's eyes were sparkling and there was a glow to her face that Nicci hadn't seen in years.

"Don't tell me you bought more horses," she said with amazement.

Geraldine smiled impishly. "Two colts. Two paints! They're not a year old yet and they're half brothers from the same father."

Since she'd only been going through the motions of eating, anyway, Nicolette put down her fork and rose from the table. "All right. Let's go see these darlings of yours."

"Well, you don't have to get in that big a hurry. Finish your supper first. Cordero is just now getting them settled anyway."

Nicolette shook her head. "I'm finished with supper. I wasn't very hungry." She looped her arm through Geraldine's and headed them both out the back door of the kitchen. "Now tell me about your day," she said. "Did you have a good time with the senator?"

As the two women walked across the patio, Geraldine sighed dreamily. "Nicci, I truly enjoyed every minute of today. Wolfe was a complete gentleman. And best of all, he made me laugh."

Nicolette glanced over at her. "Sounds like you had a good time. I'm glad." Her eyes narrowed keenly as she studied her mother's face. "Could this be the start of something serious?"

For the first time in Nicolette's memory, her mother blushed. "Oh, Nicci, I honestly can't say where this might lead. I need to know him better and he's such a busy man. Being out like this for a whole day is something he rarely gets to do."

The two of them had crossed the back lawn and were now walking on the beaten trail that led down to the same large barn where Nicolette and Ridge had gotten their mounts.

"I'm sure," Nicolette replied. "Politicians are on call just like doctors. Their schedules are demanding."

"But worthwhile," Geraldine added, then reaching over, she patted Nicci's arm. "Even though I wish you had a houseful of kids needing you, rather than a waiting room full of patients."

Nicolette didn't reply. The mention of children had her thoughts turning to little David Delaney. Seeing Ridge handling the baby with such loving hands had struck her deeply. There was no doubt in her mind that he'd be a wonderful father. But to her children? She was kidding herself to think he might ever want to take their relationship that far. She was thirty-eight years old. Even if she did look good enough to turn his head for a brief affair, that was a far cry from viewing her as a potential mother for his children.

They found Cordero and the two yearlings in a pen connected to the back of the barn. The small area was shaded by a huge live oak tree and equipped with an automatic watering trough. As Nicolette and her mother approached the fence, the two colts left Cordero's side and trotted over to them with eager whinnies.

"That's about right," Cordero spoke up with a grin. "I always lose my buddies when good-looking women show up."

Nicolette's younger cousin, Cordero San-chez, had been in charge of the horse management of the Sandbur for several years now. He was a tall, lean guy with wavy black hair and a face as handsome as all get-out. But in spite of his good looks, Nicolette knew it was his teasing charm that made him a hit with the ladies. So far he'd been gun-shy about walking down the aisle, even though his older brother, Matt, had married only a few months ago.

"I wanted Nicci to take a look at my babies," Geraldine told him, then asked, "What do you think about them, Cordero?"

All three of them knew it didn't matter what he thought about the colts. Geraldine was set on having them. But she obviously valued her nephew's opinion. Otherwise Cordero wouldn't be managing the multi-million-dollar horse sales the ranch yielded every year.

He chuckled. "Not bad for grade horses. They've got nice big bones. They'll be good for using at round-up when rough riding is needed."

Stunned, Nicolette looked at her mother. "You bought grade horses? I've never known you to do something like this."

The older woman frowned at her daughter. "Not every good horse is a registered animal, Nicci. Besides, these two had already been weaned from their mamas and they had to have a good home."

The two colts were handsome, their coats splotched with white and dark brown. Both were extremely endearing, but without having registered papers they would never be worth a whole lot monetarily.

"Why, Mother, I think the senator must

have softened your heart today," Nicci teased.

"That's what I was thinking," Cordero added with an impish grin. "Aunt Geraldine goes off on a date and comes back with two orphan colts. Next time it might be a husband."

Enjoying the banter, Geraldine laughed. "Speak for yourself, Cordero. One of these days you're going to go off on a horse buying trip and come back with a wife."

Slapping a hand across his heart, he staggered backward. "Nicci, hurry and give your mother a pill from your little black bag. My aunt is obviously sick."

Nicolette tried to laugh with her cousin, but the most she could do was give him a wry smile. "A pill won't cure love, Cordero."

Otherwise she would have taken one after the very first kiss Ridge Garroway had planted on her lips.

Chapter Eleven

Late the next evening, Ridge was sitting at the kitchen table, helping Corey with algebra homework, when the sound of a car engine and Enoch's barking interrupted their work.

"That's probably Nicci. I'll go see." As Ridge rose from his seat at the table, he pointed to the paper lying in front of the teenager. "You finish the equation."

By the time he stepped onto the verandah, Nicolette had parked her car by the yard fence and was passing through the gate. With a wide smile on his face, he trotted out to meet her.

"You're here. Finally," he said as he

swooped her up in a tight hug that lifted her completely off her feet.

By the time he'd set her back down she was laughing. "I think I'm all here," she told him as she smoothed down the skirt of her pale-pink sheathe.

Grabbing both of her hands, he walked backward while leading her toward the house. "I tried to call you this evening to make sure you were still coming. Your receptionist said you'd already gone for the day."

"I had several chores to do away from the clinic," she explained.

By now they'd reached the steps to the verandah, and he paused before leading her the rest of the way. "I was afraid that maybe you wouldn't show up," he confessed.

Surprised by the serious look on his face, she asked, "Why? I told you I would."

He shrugged. "Yes. But after I had to cancel because of work, I figured you might be…well, peeved with me."

She squeezed his hands. "Ridge, how could I be peeved with you for doing your job? You're a doctor. You're supposed to be committed to saving lives."

"Yes, but I don't want to disappoint you."

A sense of déjà vu suddenly crept over her.

Many times she'd said those very words to Bill. She'd felt guilty about being away from him while she cared for the sick. As a result she'd bent over backward in other ways to make up for their lost time together. But in the end she'd been wasting her effort and her love. He'd used her busy work schedule as a reason to have affairs.

Turning her mind away from that dark memory, she quickly assured him, "You didn't disappointment me. But I did miss you."

With a little groan he tugged her forward and placed a quick but hungry kiss on her lips. "Corey is inside finishing up his homework," he said. "Let's go in."

Moments later, as the two adults entered the kitchen, Corey looked up from his Algebra book. The moment he spotted Nicolette he politely rose to his feet.

"Evening, Miss Nicci," he greeted.

"Good evening to you, Corey," she replied. "How is the homework coming?"

With a lopsided grin, he scratched the top of his head in contemplation. "Mr. Ridge says I'm getting better. But I'm not so sure about that. Guess I'll find out when the teacher gives us another test."

Nicolette smiled with encouragement. "Bet you ace it."

Blushing furiously, Corey glanced over to Ridge. "You're sure lucky, Mr. Ridge, to have such a pretty girlfriend who's also nice. Most of the pretty ones have their noses up in the air."

Laughing, Ridge touched a forefinger to Nicolette's nose. "You think so?" he asked Corey. "Well, apparently you haven't found the right kind of pretty one yet. But you will."

Embarrassed now, Corey started to jam the homework paper into his book. "Better be going," he mumbled in a rush.

"Not just yet," Ridge ordered. "I need to look over that last problem to make sure you've done it right."

Walking over to the table, Ridge picked up the teenager's homework and began to scan the last equation on the page.

Nicolette said in a teasing voice, "Looks like Ridge is a real taskmaster."

Corey's shrug belied the great fondness she saw in his eyes. "Mr. Ridge is taking care of me," he said.

Yes, Nicolette could see that. The man was a giver. He'd already given to her in ways she could never express to him.

"Mr. Ridge takes care of a lot of people," she said softly, then quietly stepped away from the two of them as her throat tightened with emotion.

A few moments later Ridge assured Corey that the homework was correct, and the teenager gave them a quick goodbye and headed out the door.

Once the two of them were alone, Ridge gathered her into his arms. "I thought this moment would never get here," he whispered against her lips. "Do you know how good it feels to have you next to me again?"

She curled her arms around his waist and held him tightly. "I have a faint clue," she whispered back.

He rubbed his lips back and forth across hers in a teasing way. "Have you eaten?" he asked.

The warmth of his body was already making hers hum with anticipation. "No. Have you?"

"No. Should we have supper?"

Her lips tilted into a sensuous smile. "Actually, I think we should have each other."

"My, my, woman, how you read my mind," he said and then with a needy groan he picked her up and carried her to the bedroom.

Once he set her down next to the bed, there was nothing slow or hesitant about their movements. Clothes and shoes were quickly shed and tossed out of the way before they lay together in the darkness.

His mouth ravaged the tender skin of her throat, making her voice raw with desire. "I missed you. I missed this." Tilting her head back, she closed her eyes as sweet pleasure rushed through her. "You're turning me into a wanton hussy."

His hands worshipped her body as they skimmed over the pert mounds of her breasts, the valley of her belly and down her long, lean thighs. "As long as you only have eyes for me," he said with a soft chuckle.

If she lived to be ninety she would never meet another man who could touch her this way or lift her senses to the sky, she thought with certainty. Just being in his arms and having her cheek next to the beat of his heart was enough to fill her with emotions so full, so deep that she thought she would surely burst from them.

In response to his reply, she hummed a bar of the tune that matched his words, and her strained attempt had them both laughing. Until he fastened his lips over hers in a kiss that spoke of the need surging through both of them.

Once he finally raised his head, she urged, "Love me, Ridge."

"Always, sweetheart. Always."

Much, much later, after their passion had been momentarily quenched, Nicolette lay with her back and hips spooned against the curve of Ridge's warm body. His fingers slid lazily up and down her thigh and the hypnotic movement added to the pleasant drowsiness settling over her.

"My mother called again this evening," he said.

"Mmm. How did that go?"

"I told her that I had found the woman I was going to marry."

It took a moment for his reply to actually sink in. She searched for his face in the darkness. "You told her—that?"

His hand closed around her upper arm as though he expected her to bolt from the bed. "My mother and I might not see things in the same way, but I've always been honest with her. When she asked me if I'd been dating, I told her about you."

Nicolette's head was spinning. She didn't know whether to laugh or cry, or simply run out of the room and never stop running. "Dating is one thing," she exclaimed. "You said something—about marriage!"

His hand soothed the hair away from her forehead. "That's right. Surely you're not surprised to hear me say the word. Do you think I'd be here with you like this if I wasn't thinking about a future with you?"

Her heart was suddenly jumping for joy while the rest of her was frozen with fear. "I don't know. I've been—trying not to think about any of that," she admitted in a strained voice.

"Oh, Nicci," he said with a groan of frustration. "Don't try to fool me or yourself. You're not the type of woman who goes to bed with a man just for the sake of sex. Are you?"

Ever since they'd made love for the first time, Nicolette had been asking herself that very question. She'd tried to tell herself there was nothing wrong with having a purely sexual relationship with a man. After all, they were both grown-up, unattached adults. What could be the harm? Yet deep down she'd known it was her heart that had been leading her to Ridge, not her body.

"No," she whispered.

His fingers tangled themselves in the

damp strands of her long hair. "Then you do care for me."

He'd said it as a statement rather than a question. As though he wasn't going to give her the chance to deny his words. The fact left her feeling cornered, and her heart began to beat at a terrifying pace.

"Yes, I suppose I do," she admitted.

A long sigh of relief pushed past his lips. He drew her to his chest and clutched her tightly. "Oh, Nicci, I know you're afraid of this connection between us. But I love you. I want you to be my wife."

Nicolette squeezed her eyes shut as tears brimmed over the lids and rolled onto her cheeks. Why hadn't she met this man years ago when her heart was still pure and eager and she'd looked to the future with hope?

Her voice small and raspy, she said, "You can't love me, Ridge—not like that. You don't know me. Not really. We've only been together a short time."

"How long does it take a person to fall in love, Nicci? Days? Weeks? Months? From what I've seen, some people go for years—their whole lives—and never fall in love. Do you have the actual timetable requirements for this?"

Annoyed by his response, she rolled from his embrace and sat up on the side of the bed. Across from her, Ridge did the same and switched on the bedside lamp.

"You're not making this easy, are you?" she finally asked.

Walking around to her side of the bed, he eased down next to her and reached for her hand. She had to fight the urge to cry as his fingers threaded themselves between hers.

"No," he answered. "And don't expect me to let up on you. We—the two of us—are going to be married. We're going to live here as man and wife and fill this house with children. That's the way I see the future."

How many times had she imagined that very thing, Nicolette asked herself. The whole idea would be an answer to all the dreams and prayers she'd ever had. But to even allow herself to hope for such a life and then have it all crumble before her eyes would be more than her tattered heart could stand.

Numb with pain, she laid her hand against the side of his cheek. "My dear Ridge, you're not thinking clearly. You're a doctor. I'm a doctor. Our schedules are consumed with work. Last night was a good example. Trying to make a marriage succeed around our hours would be insane. Besides, I'm thirty-eight years old. You're only twenty-nine."

A scowl drew his brows into a perplexed line. "What does that have to do with anything?"

She sighed. "I only have a few child-bearing years left, Ridge. You have many. And I'm going to be way ahead of you in the aging department. After a few years I would seem like…an old woman to you. I couldn't bear that. I couldn't bear for you to turn your sights to someone younger."

"Hell and damnation! I'm not your ex-husband!"

He reached to the floor for his shorts and jerked them on. Watching him, Nicolette realized she couldn't very well argue her case in a state of nudity, especially if he was clothed.

Snatching up her strewn garments, she began to yank them on. "I didn't say you were like him," she pointed out as she tugged bra straps onto her shoulders. "But you are a man."

His arms folded across his chest as he studied her through narrowed eyes. "So that naturally makes me a bastard?"

After pulling a scanty pair of panties over her hips, she stepped into the pink sheath she'd worn to work. While she struggled with the zipper at the back, she looked at him through a tangle of dark hair. "No. It just means that… some of you become dissatisfied."

Quickly he closed the small distance between them and looked down at her with a fierce expression. "I don't know what sort of man your husband was, Nicolette. So far you haven't wanted to share that part of your past with me. But if he hurt you as you've implied, then I have to believe he was worthless. If that's what—"

"I'm not accusing—" She tried to interrupt only to stop when he turned his back to her and lifted his face toward the ceiling.

"You don't understand the sort of man I really am, Nicci. If I vowed to God to love you until death parted us, that's the way it would be. That's the sort of fiber that knits me together. Of course you're going to grow old and gravity is going to do its damage. Do you think I'm always going to look like I do now?" He turned back around and snared her gaze with his. "God willing we'll both grow old together. And during that time there would be no turning or looking to other women. It would only be you. Always."

There was such ardent conviction in his

voice that tears glazed her eyes. More than anything she wanted to fall into his arms and tell him how much she loved him. For she did love him; to tell herself anything else would be futile.

"Ridge, I...I'm sorry if I insulted you. I didn't mean to. I'm just—" She looked at him, her eyes imploring him to understand. "I only want to make you see that marrying me would be the wrong thing for both of us."

His hands curved over the tops of her shoulders, and she felt herself wilting like a morning glory after the sun has risen.

"So you say, Nicci. I happen to think we were meant for each other."

A keening, hopeless pain ripped through the center of her being. If only she could believe him. If only she had the courage to shed the dark hours of hell and self-doubt that she'd lived through during the past years. But there wasn't a brave bone left in her body. Another man had already crushed them.

Her voice strained with misery, she said, "All right. Maybe our age difference wouldn't be a problem. But there's still the fact that we're doctors. And if I was ever crazy enough to marry again, I'd be even crazier to marry a doctor. If we did have children, would you be around to help me raise them? I just can't see it. Your job or your family would suffer."

A stunned look came over his face, and then his jaws snapped together like an iron trap. Nicolette realized she'd let her tongue run away with her, but she was feeling desperate, and if making him angry made him see reality then she'd done her job.

"Well, well, isn't that something," he muttered with harsh sarcasm. "When I first met you, I distinctly remember you giving me the impression that a doctor must devote himself solely to his patient or he wasn't worth a grain of salt. And you know something, I was so enamored with you I almost wanted to work night and day just to impress you." He stepped into his jeans and jerked up the zipper. "But thank God I didn't let you sway me to that point!"

Nicolette watched him gather up his shirt and yank it over his shoulders. She realized she'd woken a sleeping lion, and she was trembling at the thought of how deep his bite might sink into her. She wanted to say something in defense of her argument, anything to take away the pain and anger she saw on his face, but words wouldn't come. Her throat was thick with tears and all she could think was that for the second time in her life she'd made a grave mistake and allowed herself to fall in love.

He walked over to her, and Nicolette cringed as his dark eyes bored into hers.

"I made a pact with myself a long time ago, Nicci, long before I ever knew you. I swore to myself that I would never be like my grandfather and my father, men who scarcely took the time for a second glance at their wives and sons. I vowed I would never let my job mean more to me than my family. And now, after all the years of schooling and the labor of getting my own practice started, I'm still not going to allow being a doctor to ruin my chances of having a loving wife and a houseful of children. If you don't believe me about this, Nicolette, then maybe the two of us *are* wrong for each other."

She swallowed the painful emotions that were lodged in her throat. "I don't doubt that you mean to keep your career and your marriage balanced. I believe you're speaking from your heart. But—" She paused as the sting of tears grew larger and larger until wet tracks finally rolled down her cheeks.

"Things change, Ridge. Sometimes well-meaning intentions are shoved aside, along with people's feelings. I don't want us to do that to each other. Believe it or not, I want what's best for you."

Knowing she couldn't push another word through her aching throat, she grabbed up her high heels and walked out of the bedroom on shaky legs.

Ridge followed her to the front door. "I guess this means you're leaving," he said flatly.

Her head twisted so that she was looking over her shoulder at him. "Yes," she said hoarsely.

His nostrils flared as he drew in a deep breath. "Why? And don't give me all those reasons I just heard, Nicci. I'm not stupid. I can put two and two together, just like any other man when he's been taken for a ride. Having a fling with me was okay, but living here on this small property, in this old house, day in, day out, is a bit too much for you to stomach. Especially someone like you, who's used to opulent surroundings and maids to do your bidding." A sneer twisted his lips. "Well, I *could* give you those things, Nicci. We Garroways have money, too. But that's not the way I want to live. And I don't want a woman I have to buy!"

His words struck her like stones being flung from a slingshot. She was so stunned by the sudden pain that for long moments all she could do was stare at him. Then finally her head swung slowly back and forth in disbelief.

"This has been a mistake," she whispered in a crushed voice. "Everything between us has been a mistake."

Not bothering to put on her heels, she scurried through the door, across the porch and out to her car. Along the way, she caught a glimpse of Enoch lifting his head from his bed of grass and watching her with faint curiosity. But the dog didn't bother to follow her and neither did Ridge.

As she started the engine she could see his tall form silhouetted in the open door of the house. Her heart awash with tears, she pulled the gearshift into reverse. At the same time, she saw his hand lift from its place on the doorjamb, and for one split second, one hopeful moment, she thought he was going to gesture for her to come back, or at the very least, lift his hand in farewell to her.

But he did neither of those things. Instead he closed the door and shut her completely from his sight.

Chapter Twelve

Two weeks later, Ridge was sitting in his office, staring out at the growing twilight blanketing the parking lot and the adjoining city park. All of his patients were gone and so was his staff. It was time for him to be heading home, too. But he couldn't seem to gather enough will to leave the room.

His office was the only place that Nicolette's presence didn't consume him. At home he could hardly go into any room without being struck by her image, especially in his bedroom where the two of them had made love so passionately. Hell, he guessed the best thing he could do now would be to move his things into another bedroom. Maybe then he'd be able to lie down and sleep instead of staring at the walls until the small hours of the morning, torturing himself with thoughts of what might have been.

For the past few days he'd been asking himself over and over how he could have been so mistaken about Nicolette. He thought he'd learned his lesson with Brittany. She'd also led him on a merry chase, and when he'd finally caught her, she'd laughed at his idea of a home on the range with children underfoot. Maybe one of these days he'd use better judgment in the way of women.

With an audible groan, Ridge turned away from the plate-glass window and started back to his desk. Hell, there wasn't any use planning to meet another woman. He wasn't going to be looking for one. He didn't want another one. Nicolette had made sure of that.

Love for her still burned in his heart like a bright, eternal flame. The only thing that would end its fire would be for him to quit breathing.

At the corner of his desk stood a stack of charts belonging to the patients he would be seeing tomorrow. The folder lying on top was Dan Nelson's, the old wrangler who had refused to be treated by anyone but Nicolette.

Ridge had seen the older man at least two times since then. So far he'd been taking his medicine and following doctor's orders. Normally Ridge enjoyed their brief visits. He enjoyed talking with him and hearing about his latest escapades. But Dan would no doubt ask about Nicolette, and Ridge didn't want to have to explain that he'd cut his ties with her. Dan thought Nicci was an angel in a white lab coat. The whole thing was going to make for an awkward situation.

But an uncomfortable situation with a patient was nothing compared to the pain going on inside of him, Ridge thought. The worst part about it was that he didn't have a clue as to how to fix the situation, how to erase all the horrible things they'd said to each other. A thousand times these past few days he'd wanted to pick up the phone and call her. Several times he'd considered walking across the clinic to her office. At least there she couldn't refuse to see him without making a scene. But he'd not done either of those things. For whatever reason, she didn't want to make a life with him. He had to accept that fact, even if it took a hundred years to do it.

With a weary sigh, Ridge turned out the light over his desk and left the office.

The last thing he expected to find when he got home was his mother's beige Lincoln parked in front of the gate. He couldn't imagine what had brought her on the 130-mile trip from Houston. Particularly since she wasn't one to get out and travel as far as the local mall without someone with her. He only hoped to God that she was sober.

Ridge found her in the living room. She was sitting stiffly on the edge of an armchair staring in abject fear at Enoch, who was stretched out on his stomach in front of her feet. His paws were shoved together in a tight point, his nose resting on top. The dog was staring up at the strange woman with a mixture of curiosity and anticipation.

At the sight of her son, Lillian wilted with relief. "He—" she pointed to the German shepherd "—barged his way past my legs and into the house! I thought he was going to maul me!"

Ridge mentally shook his head. Enoch was a baby. He didn't know the meaning of the word *bite*. "You mean with his tongue?" Ridge asked with wry humor. "Enoch loves everyone."

"Not me!" She brushed at the invisible hairs on her linen slacks. "I don't like dogs and they don't like me!"

Enoch's ears shot forward, and then he rose to his feet and slunk away from the visitor as though he'd figured her out and didn't like the company.

Ridge bent down and gave his pet a scruffy pat on the head. "Mmm. Guess you got that point over," he said to his mother, then, bending down toward the dog, he said, "Enoch, you go to the kitchen and eat your treats."

The dog obediently trotted out of the room, and Ridge walked over to his mother. He pressed a kiss on a cheek that was perfectly rouged and powdered. Her short hair was streaked with just enough blond to hide the gray, and the lines around her eyes were carefully camouflaged with makeup. He wondered how soon it would be before she headed to a plastic surgeon. Lillian's looks were more important to her than even her husband's money, and that was saying a mouthful.

She smiled up at him, but he could see the expression didn't reach her eyes. The same sense of sad defeat that he remembered from the last time they were together was still etched upon her features. Ridge hated her beaten attitude, and he couldn't help but compare her sourness to Geraldine Saddler's optimistic warmth.

"This is quite a surprise, Mother. Have you been here long?"

"Only a few minutes. I tried ringing your cell, but you must have turned it off."

Since he wasn't on hospital call tonight, Ridge had indeed turned off the cell phone. He'd not been in the mood to talk to anyone. But it looked as though his mother had changed his plans for a quiet evening.

"Would you like something to eat or drink?" he offered.

Her manicured fingers fiddled absently with the chunky gold necklace draped against the oyster silk blouse she was wearing. On the outside she was still a beautiful woman, but what really mattered to him was the inside. He'd often sought and hoped to find a measure of compassion in his mother. It was there, deep down in a place where she would let no one see. Not even him.

The corners of her lips turned downward as she glanced around the modest living room. "I don't suppose you have any Scotch."

"No. But I do have some chilled beer," he said.

"Beer! That's a blue-collar drink, Ridge. Don't tell me this place has already made your standards sink."

There used to be a time that Lillian's snide remarks would bring his temper to the boiling point. But down through the years he'd realized getting angry with her was pointless. Now she simply left him feeling weary.

"I've been drinking beer for years, Mother. It's my spirit of choice." Actually, he had a bottle of wine and another bottle of tequila stored away in the kitchen just in case he wanted to offer a guest a margarita or a glass of Chardonnay. But his mother didn't need the alcohol. She seemed to be perfectly sober at the moment and he didn't want to risk sending her off on a binge. "I'll just make us some coffee. Would you like to come into the kitchen with me? Or stay where you are?"

"I'll come with you. Just in case that mongrel decides to jump on me." She rose to her feet and brushed the seat of her slacks as though she expected dirt and dog hair to fall to the floor. "I didn't realize you even owned a dog."

He took her by the arm and escorted her toward the kitchen. "I've told you about him. You probably weren't listening."

"Oh, Ridge," she scolded in a sugary drawl. "You know your mother has lots of things on her mind. I can't remember everything you tell me."

In the kitchen he pulled out a chair for her at the small dinette and, after getting her settled, went to work making a pot of coffee. Once it was dripping, he walked over to where she sat and rested a hip against the table's edge. Across the room Enoch was curled into a large, furry ball, pretending to be asleep, but Ridge could see one of the dog's eyes was cracked and carefully watching Lillian's movements.

"You told me you would never come to this place, Mom. What changed your mind?"

Crossing her legs, she smoothed the material of her slacks over her knee. "To be honest, I gave up on you. I thought I could wait you out and you'd soon return to Houston. Now I realize more drastic measures are needed."

His brows lifted with sardonic disbelief. "To get me to return to Houston? Drastic won't do it. Nothing will. This is my home now. I've told you that."

Her toe tapped the air in a frustrated rhythm. "You haven't even asked about your father," she said with a hint of censure. "Don't you care about him?"

Ridge felt everything in him tighten into a defensive stance. "I used to care, Mother. When I was six, seven, even ten years old, I cared about the man. I would have given my right arm for one hour of his attention. Now I simply think of him and wonder about the wasteful choices he's made in his life."

Lillian's gaze darted away from her son and he realized she didn't want him to see the shadows of regret on her face. "Oh, Ridge," she said in a small, plaintive voice, "do you always have to analyze everyone? People are human. We make mistakes. And I'm sure your father is aware that he's made a few."

Ridge's cynical laugh followed him as he walked back to the counter and poured two mugs of coffee. "Let's not discuss the old man, Mother. I'm not up to it tonight."

Back at the table he placed the coffee in front of her, along with cream, sugar and a teaspoon.

While she doctored the drink with both condiments, she studied her son with a keen eye. "You do look drained, dear. Have a bad day?"

No, he'd just gone through the worst week of his life, he thought. He couldn't eat. Sleep came to him in fitful dozes and his mind was a useless pool of misery. Ridge understood he had to hold on to his faith and remind himself that things would get better, but he wondered where he could possibly look for the light that Nicolette had taken away. How could he get it—and her—back?

"Things have been…stressful here lately. I'll be all right." He sank into the chair opposite hers. "What do you think of my house?"

Ridge realized asking the question was the same as asking to be beaten with a baseball bat, but he'd never been one to tiptoe around his mother, and he wasn't about to start now.

"Well, I took a look around the rooms before you got home." She shot him a helpless look as she lifted the coffee mug to her lips. "I suppose it's okay for a hunting cabin. But really, Ridge, you don't expect to continue to live here like this. It's a common farmhouse, and an old one at that!"

"I'm not a hunter, Mom. I'm a rancher. This is just the sort of place I need to get a herd started."

Clutching her coffee mug, Lillian rolled her eyes with obvious disgust. "A rancher! Cows and horses! I've heard that stuff from you since you were a little boy. And I blame Barry for this ridiculous obsession you have to be a cowboy. I should never have allowed you to become friends with him in the first place. The Macons didn't understand your upbringing. They're the sort of people who just do whatever they can to get by in the world. You, on the other hand, have a calling."

His nostrils flaring with disgust, he said, "You couldn't have stopped me from spending time with the Macons. Barry is like my brother. A brother I should have had but didn't."

She looked away from him, and just for a split second Ridge thought he'd glimpsed remorse on her face. Hell, he must be in such a desolate state of mind he was starting to get delusional. He'd never seen his mother remorseful over anything.

"Barry was a bad influence," she went on, but her voice softened just a tad. "Your birthright was to be a doctor and nothing else. Certainly not a man who gets manure on his hands!"

"Doctors do have lives outside of the clinic," he said dryly. At least, he'd had one until Nicolette had turned his world upside down. He missed her so much his body literally ached. "But I can see that's something you haven't realized yet."

Lillian looked at him sharply and opened her mouth to say something, then seemed to think better of it. After a couple sips of coffee she changed the subject completely. "I've been thinking about what you told me the other day. About the woman you've met."

Ridge hoped the pain in his heart wasn't written on his face. He wasn't about to tell his mother that Nicolette had dumped him. Lillian's triumph would simply be too much for him to take. Besides, he wasn't going to roll over and forget the woman he loved. Somehow, some way, he was going to bring them back together.

Cautiously he asked, "And what have you been thinking? I hope you're happy for me."

"Happy?" she practically shrieked, then, clutching her throat with her hand, she let out a mocking laugh. "Ridge, you can't be serious. Do you honestly think your father and I had our dreams set on you marrying a divorcee? It's downright scandalous. And you surely knew that we'd see it that way before you ever started the relationship. But you probably didn't give a damn. You never do."

Ridge simply stared at her and waited for her to get the tirade out of her system.

"Well?" she eventually prodded. "Don't you have anything to say for yourself? Please tell me that you've changed your mind about this woman. I can't imagine inviting my friends to the wedding. They'd all be whispering behind their hands, laughing at me. Especially when they know you could have any Houston debutante you laid your eyes on. But, oh no, that would be too right, too easy for you. You've got to buck tradition no matter who it hurts." Bending her head, she pretended to be fighting off tears. "You're my only child, Ridge. I've always dreamed of seeing you married in a splendid ceremony to a woman with an old, respected name."

Rising from the table, Ridge walked over to the sink and poured the dregs of his coffee down the drain.

With his back to his mother he said, "I've always dreamed about marrying a woman I love. But I guess that's a novel idea for you and Father."

She gasped. "Ridge!"

Turning, he leveled a look on her that was too fierce for her to ignore. "Listen closely,

Mother, because I'm not going to say this again. Nothing and no one is going to make me return to Houston."

Rising to her feet, Lillian rushed over to him. "But, Ridge, your father's practice is—"

"I would give up being a doctor completely before I'd work in his office! Richard Garroway is a selfish adulterer! Why don't you face up to the fact that he doesn't care anything about you or me? He never has." He slashed a hand through the air. "Oh, he cares about appearances and how he can use them to his advantage, but that's where his caring stops. And if you ever decide you want something real in your life, you'll get out of this farce you call a marriage!"

Lillian stared at him in utter shock and then her whole presence appeared to crumble. Tears filled her eyes, but this time Ridge could see that they were real rather than crocodile. He felt bad about his outburst, but she couldn't keep living in denial and smothering her pain and loneliness with cocktails.

"Ridge. Ridge. You don't understand," she muttered miserably. "Don't you think I know about Richard? That I've known about his philandering for years?"

Ridge looked at her with faint surprise. "Then why didn't you do something about it?"

Her head wagged slowly back and forth in defeat. "Because I didn't have the courage. It was easier for me to pretend that everything was okay. But deep down I knew everything was really broken. Richard only married me because of my family's money. I'm sure you've already figured that out for yourself. And afterward, well, I was so young and impressionable. I liked having a handsome husband with a brilliant career. It was so much more than most of my friends had, or so I believed all those years ago. Over the years I've begun to see it was really…so much less. I try so hard to pretend that everything is lovely—that's why I have to have the alcohol, to be able to forget, to be able to pretend. But most of the time—when I'm alone and sober as I am now—I feel like my life is over."

Seeing the awful pain exposed on her face, Ridge put his arm around her shoulders and drew her to him. "Oh, Mother, I love you. Surely you've always known that, too. And I want you to have a happy life. A real life. That will never happen unless you find the courage to make a move."

"A move—oh, my son," she said in a choked voice. "It's too late for that."

He lifted her chin with his forefinger and gave her a soft smile of encouragement. "You're only fifty-three years old, Mom. That's still very young. You have plenty of time to start over. And there are lots of men out there willing to marry a divorcee if he believes she'll make him happy."

Easing her cheek away from his chest, she looked up and tried to smile through her tears. "You make it sound so easy. But it isn't, Ridge. Not when you're afraid to try again. And for so many years your father has controlled me. I don't know how to do anything. I never tried to do anything on my own because your father refused to let me. He always said I was his queen and I wasn't to lift a hand. But I finally figured out that was only Richard's charming way of keeping me under his thumb."

Just hearing his mother admit that she had problems felt like a miracle, and Ridge squeezed her shoulders with hopeful support. Maybe this would be the turning point that he'd often prayed his mother would come to.

"Just promise me that you'll try, Mom. And I'll be here for you. Okay?"

Too choked to speak, she nodded and wiped at the tears that were now smearing her mascara. Ridge handed her a napkin and as she wiped at her eyes, he said, "When you were looking around the house, you probably noticed, I have two extra bedrooms. I'd really like for you to spend the night. Will you?"

Lillian let out a shaky laugh. "Well, why not? When I was a little girl I used to wonder what it would be like to stay on a ranch. Tonight I'm finally going to find out."

Three days later Sunday settled over the Sandbur with a steamy heat that was only relieved by a lazy breeze that bothered to drift now and then over the quiet ranch yard. Nicolette spent most of the day in her bedroom, going through the motions of trying to rest and read, but never succeeding at either.

More than two weeks had passed since she'd run like a scared, wounded animal from Ridge's house. For the first few days she'd licked her wounds and told herself she deserved the pain. She'd been stupid for allowing herself to get that close to danger. But she'd been charmed and lonely and she'd believed she could enjoy being with him without getting hurt.

How stupid could she have been? Did she really think she could fall into his arms, be in his bed and not fall in love with him?

Groaning with misery, Nicolette stared out her bedroom window. All was quiet and serene beneath the arms of the spreading live oaks. Songbirds flittered from the grass to the trees while two yellow cur dogs slept in the heat of the evening.

The peaceful scene was a huge contrast to the turmoil in her heart and, as she'd done a thousand times these past few days, she wondered what she could do, how she could change this misery she'd brought on herself.

She'd not told any of her family about her broken relationship with Ridge. For one thing she doubted they could understand the full extent of her misery. Not without knowing the utter, complete love she felt for the man. And what would be the use of admitting that to anyone, she asked herself, when she'd already ruined everything between the two of them.

Her restless heart pushed her around the room until she was practically pacing. Maybe if she talked to her sister, she could make sense of this misery she was going through, Nicolette thought. But Mercedes was stationed on the tiny island of Diego Garcia in the Indian Ocean. Her duties with the Air Force were secret at the moment, and it was an ordeal to make phone connections with her. Crying on Mercedes's shoulder was impossible right now.

Juliet, her cousin Matt's wife, was a good listener and Nicolette loved the other woman deeply. But Juliet and Matt were practically newlyweds and their love for each other was so obvious it was almost painful for Nicolette to see. Plus Juliet was pregnant, something that Nicolette had so ardently wanted for herself. No, talking to Juliet would only remind Nicolette of everything she was losing with Ridge, and that was the last thing she needed to lift her out of this black cloud.

Feeling boxed in by the walls of her room and her own wretchedness, Nicolette went out to the kitchen.

Cook had retired for the evening, and the room was quiet with everything in its place. The sight of the kitchen had Nicolette's thoughts turning to Ridge's place and how he'd accused her of thinking the house wasn't good enough for her to live in. He believed she wanted maids and a cook to do her bidding, as though she was so spoiled she couldn't care for herself or him. The accusation had probably hurt her more than anything he'd said. So much so that for the past few days she'd wanted to march down to his office and tell him how the cow ate the corn. She wanted him to know exactly how wrong he was about her.

But to do that would only stir up the ashes again and Nicolette needed to let them die. She needed to forget about Ridge Garroway and get on with this solitary life she'd made for herself.

Chapter Thirteen

Minutes later Nicolette fixed herself a glass of sweet iced tea with lemon and then headed out the door of the kitchen with the intention of drinking the cold beverage on the patio.

Outside she was quietly fastening the screen door behind her when the voices of her mother and brother floated over to her.

"I really don't know what's happened," Geraldine was saying. "She hasn't said anything to me."

Suspecting that the "she" her mother was talking about was her, Nicolette paused in her tracks and listened.

Lex quickly replied, "Well, I've never seen her looking so unhappy. It's got to be that young doctor who's caused her all this grief. For two cents I'd go look him up and beat the hell out of him."

"Lex, Lex," Geraldine scolded with sarcasm. "This isn't Dodge City."

"Hell, no! We're not in Kansas. We're in Texas, thank God. And down here we take care of our own! I may not be Matt Dillon, but I sure as hell can handle Dr. Garroway."

Nicolette shook her head while she heard her mother groan with disapproval.

"Really, Lex! In spite of what you think, there are ways other than fists to settle a matter. Besides, this isn't any of your business. This is Nicolette's life. Not yours."

"Mom, do you think I want to see my sister hurt? It kills me to see her acting as though there's no tomorrow. She's already carrying around enough of the miserable baggage Bill left her with. Now she's gone and let another man stab a stake in her heart."

Was that the way she appeared to her family, Nicolette wondered? As though she was a hopeless judge of men? The idea shocked and angered her. She didn't want their pity!

Marching across the patio to where Lex and their mother were sitting, Nicolette glanced from one to the other.

"What are you two doing out here discussing me?" she demanded.

Unperturbed by her curt tone, Lex asked, "What are you doing out here eavesdropping?"

"I came out to drink my tea in peace. Instead, I find you two discussing me as though I need to be put away before I hook myself up with another loser!"

"Oh, Nicci," Geraldine gently admonished. "We don't think any such thing! We're only worried about you. We don't even know if Ridge is your problem. Since you've clammed up, we can only guess."

Embarrassed by her defensive outburst, Nicolette sighed and sank down next to her brother, who was rocking gently back and forth in a cedar glider.

"I'm sorry," she mumbled. "I understand you two care about me. It's just that—I feel like an idiot for letting this thing with Ridge get me down."

"What thing?" Lex prodded.

Geraldine looked expectantly at her daughter.

Nicolette sighed again. "We had a big rift a few days back and I left his place. We haven't spoken since."

"What sort of rift?" Geraldine asked. "I'm sure it's something that can be fixed."

Nicolette glumly shook her head. "I don't think so. Ridge asked me to marry him. I refused."

"What! Oh God in heaven, why?" Geraldine asked in dismay.

Lex shoved a hand in the air. "Now just wait a minute, Mom. We all know that you want your babies married and happy. But you need to hear Nicolette's side of things before you start in on her about this. After all, you just said this was sissy's business, not ours."

Geraldine scowled at her son. "I might have known you'd side with your sister. A damn mule couldn't drag you down the marriage aisle. But maybe that's a good thing 'cause I doubt any decent woman could put up with you." She turned her attention back to Nicolette. "And as for you, Nicci, I just don't understand how much longer you're going to keep running from your past. I never thought a daughter of mine would end up a coward!"

Sensing they needed to stick together against their mother's wrath, Nicolette snuggled closer to her brother while he put a comforting arm around her shoulders.

Nicolette said, "You don't understand, Mother! And neither does Ridge! We have too many years between us. Besides that, we're both doctors. Our jobs would never allow us to be together."

Unimpressed with Nicolette's reasoning, Geraldine looked at her daughter with a bit of disgust. "I've heard these arguments from you before. And if that's the way you felt, why did you get involved with the man in the first place? You knew both of you were doctors!"

Feeling utterly stupid, Nicolette's chin dropped to her chest. "Of course I did. But I believed—I thought we could be just—I thought we could be together without getting serious."

"In other words, just have an affair—enjoy the man without any strings or commitments," Geraldine muttered with distaste, then shook her head as though she couldn't believe she was discussing her own daughter's behavior. "Thank goodness Ridge wouldn't give in to you!"

Nicolette glanced up at her brother for aid and support. "Lex, tell her! Tell her that I just jumped out of a burning skillet and that

I don't want to jump into another one. Marriage to Ridge would be all wrong!"

His gaze gently roamed her face and then his hand smoothed over her dark hair. "Nicci, sweet sissy, the short time you and Ridge were together I've never seen you looking happier. I believe you love the man."

Neither her brother nor her mother could ever know how very much she did love Ridge, Nicolette thought. Even she hadn't realized the real depth of her feelings until the days without him had begun to slip by and her heart had grown emptier and emptier.

"I do love him, Lex. That's why it hurts so much to be away from him."

Across from them, Geraldine spat, "Hell! If you really felt that way about the man, you'd get over there and tell him so! You wouldn't be sitting here whining about it!"

Lex shot his mother a reproving glance. "Mom, you don't have to be so rough. Can't you see she's hurting?"

Geraldine loved her children greatly. But she was made of strong, sturdy stock and she expected her offspring to be equally as tough. It wasn't in her to allow anything less.

"I'm not blind, Lex," Geraldine told him. "And don't expect me to pat Nicci's cheek and say, 'You poor little thing, go ahead and cry and everything will be all right.' I've tried to be easy with her and that hasn't worked. Besides, that's not the Ketchum way. It's not the Saddler way either." She looked directly at Nicolette. "I'm going to say one thing on the matter and that's it. The rest is up to you, Nicci. Do you want to hear it?"

The only response Nicolette could give her was a simple nod.

Geraldine leaned forward toward her two offspring. "Love is too precious to throw away. And nothing in this world is perfect. If you think you're going to find the perfect man with just the right job so that the two of you can have a flawless marriage and dance around on a dreamy cloud, then you might as well roll over and give up right now."

After she spoke, Geraldine got up from her lawn chair and left the patio. Nicolette turned a torn gaze on her brother.

"I think she's angry with me," she murmured with regret.

Lex's smile was wan. "She loves you and she wants you to be happy. So do I."

Nicolette let out a long breath. "Do you think she's right?"

Her brother chuckled.   "Let me put it

this way, I've never seen her when she wasn't right."

Nicolette darted a glance at her mother's retreating back, then stared blindly forward as her mind swam in all directions.

After several long moments she said to herself and to Lex, "I wasn't expecting Ridge to be perfect."

"Weren't you?" he asked softly.

Jerking her head around, she stared wondrously at her brother. "No! I was trying to be logical about things."

A wan smile touched his lips. "From what I've heard, love and logic don't mix."

With an agonized groan, Nicolette covered her face with her hands. "A woman has to be careful," she tried to reason, but her heart was already beating fast, thumping out orders for her to get to her feet and fly to Ridge as swiftly as they could carry her.

"A woman has to take chances," he countered.

She looked at him for a moment and then leaped up from the swing so suddenly that it swung madly.

"Where are you going?" he called as she hurried toward the house.

"To take a chance!"

* * *

Miles away at Ridge's place, late-evening thunderclouds were gathering overhead as he and Corey headed to the barn to finish the evening chores.

After church that morning, Ridge had brought the teenager home with him. Since that time the two of them had been removing the rusty, corrugated iron from the roof of the chicken house. They'd stopped only for a light lunch and now they were dirty, hungry and tired.

"Some hamburgers and milkshakes would taste real good right now, don't you think?" Ridge asked the boy as the two of them stepped into the barn.

"Boy, yeah! And some French fries, too. Or maybe some onion rings. You know how to cook those, Mr. Ridge?"

Since Nicolette had left, Ridge hadn't done much cooking or eating. The joy of making a meal had left him, and eating was just something to keep his body from collapsing. Nothing about life was the same without her and he realized he'd reached the point where he had to do something about his misery. He couldn't go on living in that sort of agony.

"No," he answered Corey. "And I'm not going to cook this evening. We're going to drive into town and eat in a restaurant. My treat. How would that be?"

Corey paused in the act of opening the door to the feed room and turned an incredulous look on Ridge. "Really? That'd be great! Mom's at work, so she won't be around to make supper."

Suzette, Corey's mother, was forced to work long hours to support herself and her son. She had no other choice. Yet Ridge could see how much better things would be for the teenager if his mother were more available to him. Corey's family situation, or lack of one, had set Ridge to thinking about a lot of the things Nicolette had said to him that night before she'd driven away.

Now that he'd had more than enough time to think about it, most of what she'd said had held at least a measure of truth. It would be hard for the two of them to find quality time for each other and for their children. He could admit that. But nothing worthy in life was easy to obtain. He had to believe it could be done. He had to go to Nicolette and convince her that the two of them needed to be together.

During his mother's visit, Lillian had confessed to Ridge how scared she was to start over. Richard Garroway had stripped away her sense of worth and crushed her ability to trust in herself as a woman and a person. These past few days Ridge had been asking himself if the same held true for Nicolette. Maybe she was simply too scared to let herself try again.

If that was the case, he had to make her see that she could trust him with her heart, her very life.

Pulling his mind back to the task at hand, he told Corey, "I'll get the feed. You go open the gate and let the horses into the lot. And be careful."

Nodding, Corey left the cover of the building and Ridge stepped inside the feed room to collect a fifty-pound sack of sweet feed. He was in the process of ripping the top open when, outside the barn, a light flashed and thunder cracked with such a vengeance that Ridge jerked and very nearly toppled the whole contents of the sack onto the floor.

Realizing a storm was about to hit, he propped up the open sack and hurried out of the barn to check on Corey.

The teenager already had the five horses in the lot and was trying to get the gate shut, but the animals were stirred up by the approaching storm and were nudging and pressing Corey tightly against the metal gate.

Sensing that the horses were endangering his buddy, Enoch began to bark loudly and nip at their heels.

"Wave your arms, Corey! Make them get back away from you," Ridge yelled to the boy as he quickly climbed the fence. "Climb over the gate! Get out of there!"

Corey brandished an arm through the air and managed to drive one horse away. He was attempting to shoo the others to the opposite side of the pen when another streak of lightning lit up the sky. One of the animals reared up in fear and pawed the air. Another one bolted with Enoch barking frantically at his heels. Amid the chaos, the one horse that remained near Corey began to buck.

Ridge didn't see exactly how it happened, but he saw the flash of a back hoof slicing viciously toward the boy and then heard a sickening thud as it landed in the middle of his chest.

"Corey! Oh, God!"

By the time Ridge got to him, the teenager had already crumpled to the ground with his face buried in the dirt.

"Corey!"

There was no response, and Ridge swiftly but carefully eased the boy onto his back. The moment he saw that Corey wasn't breathing, fear rushed over him like a blinding wall of water.

A cell phone was in his jeans pocket, but every second was critical. They were too far away for an ambulance rescue, and he didn't want to waste the few precious moments needed to make the emergency call. Instead he ripped open Corey's shirt and laid his ear to his chest.

No heart beat. No respiration. Nothing.

Steeling himself against the personal emotions pouring through him, Ridge quickly ordered the doctor in him to take over.

One. Two. Three. He began to count the compressions he made on Corey's chest, followed by the breaths he blew into the lifeless boy's mouth and nostrils.

Over and over Ridge pumped and blew and prayed for the boy to show some sort of response. A few feet away he could hear Enoch whining a pitiful wail as though he were begging Ridge to make his little buddy okay again.

My boy! My boy! Breathe for me! Come back to me!

Ridge was growing doubtful and wondering if he should leave Corey long enough to run to the house to search for a stimulant among his stash of emergency medical supplies, when the teenager made a faint gasp for air.

Sending up a silent prayer of thanks, Ridge swiftly placed his ear once again to Corey's chest. The faint sound of heartbeat was like a heavenly trumpet to his ears.

"That's it! Hang in there, son! You're going to be all right."

With tears of relief glazing his eyes, he jerked out the cell phone and dialed 911.

By the time he'd finished giving the dispatcher his location and the reason of the emergency, rain had begun to fall in earnest and Corey had started to rouse and mumble in a disoriented way.

Ridge picked the boy up in his arms and carried him to the cover of the barn to wait for the ambulance.

After the conversation with her mother and brother, Nicolette didn't waste time changing clothes. She brushed her hair, grabbed her handbag and jumped in her car. It wasn't until she was halfway to Ridge's place that it dawned on her he might be on duty this evening and could perhaps be attending patients at the hospital.

Her cell phone was lying in the console next to her seat, but she'd not programmed the instrument with Ridge's number. And even if she remembered the set of digits, she wasn't sure she would call him. Surprise was always best when a woman was planning an attack on a man.

If she didn't find him at home, she would wait until he returned. Maybe the shock of seeing her again would catch him off guard and give her a chance to explain herself before he ordered her to leave the premises, she thought grimly.

Once she turned off the main highway to head toward Ridge's small ranch, a tropical deluge began to pour from the sky. Even with her windshield wipers on high speed, she was forced to creep along the road in order to see.

Relief washed over her when she finally spotted Ridge's turnoff, but she'd hardly had time to ease her death grip on the steering wheel before an emergency vehicle raced out of the little dirt lane and directly in front of her.

Dear God, it was an ambulance coming from Ridge's place!

Was Ridge inside, she wondered frantically, or had a guest of his become ill?

Torn between following the ambulance or driving to Ridge's house to see if he might be there, she made a quick decision to do the latter and sped her car down the rough, muddy road until she reached the yard gate.

Enoch was on the porch, but Ridge was nowhere in sight as she raced up the steps and into the house. The dog followed her and continued to whine in a soulful way as she went through the rooms calling Ridge's name.

"It's all right, Enoch," she said with a quick pat to the dog's head. "I'll find him and bring him home."

There was only one place for the ambulance to go and that was the county hospital. With her whole body trembling in fear, Nicolette raced to her car and gunned it back down the dirt lane.

Thankfully, by the time she reached the main highway, the rain had eased and she stepped down on the accelerator as much as she dared with all the water pooled in the ruts of the asphalt.

Even as the miles sped behind her, time seemed to stand still for Nicolette. Emotions, raw and painful, jabbed her from every direction and she realized she hated herself for not seeing Ridge as the man she loved, the very thing she wanted most in her life.

If something had happened to him, if she lost him before she had the chance to tell him how she really felt, she'd never be able to survive, she thought sickly.

At the hospital she parked her vehicle at the emergency entrance and raced inside to the admitting desk.

A nurse that Nicolette was acquainted with was on duty. She practically yelled at the other woman. "Joan, where's Ridge? What's happened?"

The tall blonde looked at her with mild confusion. "You mean Dr. Garroway?"

Nicolette's knees were so mushy she had to grip the edge of the desk to keep herself upright. "Yes! What's happened to him? What examining room is he in?"

The nurse's head swung back and forth. "Nothing has happened to Dr. Garroway. He came in with a patient, a young boy."

Nicolette's hand flew to her mouth. "Corey! Oh, no!"

Joan glanced at the set of papers she'd been working on. "Yes, that's his name. I think there was some sort of accident with a horse. Anyway, I believe they've already gone up to ICU with him."

"Thank you!" she called over her shoulder as she took off in a run to the elevator.

Because she was considered a part of the hospital's medical staff, she didn't pause in the waiting room but walked straight through to the nurse's station in the Intensive Care unit.

The head nurse gave her a quick rundown on Corey's condition, which she described as stable, and promised Nicolette to let her know if there were any changes.

Not wanting to cause any further interruption, Nicolette thanked the nurse and went back to the waiting area, where she practically collapsed on one of the couches. Ridge would have to appear sooner or later. In the meantime, she could only hope and pray that he wouldn't turn his back on her.

More than an hour passed before Ridge finally stepped into the waiting room. His jeans and boots were covered with dirt and splotches of mud, but he'd apparently changed his shirt for a green scrub. Weariness tugged at his features, and for a moment she feared for Corey's condition.

"Ridge! How is he?"

Unaware of her presence, he jerked his head in her direction.

"Nicci?" His eyes narrowed on her face. "What are you doing here?"

Swallowing at the lump of nerves in her throat, she left the couch and walked over to him. "I...I went to your house and saw the ambulance leaving. I followed. Is Corey—"

"He's going to be fine, thank God." Briefly closing his eyes, he raked a hand through his hair. "There for a while I wasn't sure, though. His heart stopped completely. I had to do CPR before the ambulance got there."

"Oh, Ridge," she said softly. "I can't imagine the terror you must have felt. Corey is such a sweet boy, and I know how much he means to you."

His eyes met hers with bleak certainty. "He's like my son. I don't know what I would have done if he'd died."

"How did the accident happen?"

Shaking his head, he said, "The storm was approaching and the horses got shook up from the lightning. One of them bucked and Corey was close enough that a hind hoof slammed him in the chest. The impact was so great it stopped his heart."

Nicolette had experienced a few ranching injuries herself, so it wasn't hard to imagine the horror Ridge had experienced when he'd witnessed Corey being kicked by a twelve-hundred-pound horse. "Will there be any permanent damage?" she asked.

"I don't think so. He's young and healthy, and his heart has already returned to a normal rhythm. In fact, he's complaining now for making him stay in the hospital overnight. Especially when I'd promised him a trip into town for a hamburger."

Relief flooded through her and she smiled. "I'm so glad. What about his mother? Has she been told about the accident?"

He nodded. "Suzette's in there with him now. You probably saw her come flying through here earlier." He indicated midchest height. "About this tall, red-headed with lots of freckles."

"I did see the woman and wondered if she might be Corey's mother. I'm sure she was in a panic. Were you able to reassure her?"

He wiped a hand over his strained features. "Yes. She's calm now. In fact, she kept thanking me over and over for saving her son's life." The corners of his mouth turned downward. "But I don't know how she's going to feel about things once it sinks in that Corey was hurt because of me. She may not want the boy to associate with me anymore."

Desperate to comfort him, Nicolette placed her hand on his forearm. "Accidents happen, Ridge. Especially when you mix animals and people. I'm sure Corey's mother understands that. And she must also know that you love the boy."

Faint surprise flashed in his brown eyes, then softened with gratitude. "At least you realize that I'm a man capable of loving someone other than myself."

Pain squeezed Nicolette's heart, causing her fingers to unconsciously tighten on his arm. "Ridge, I—" Shaking her head, her voice lowered as she tried again. "I need to talk to you. Can we go somewhere—" she glanced around at the weary people sitting on chairs and couches as they waited to hear the condition of loved ones "—a little more private?"

Skepticism marked his face as he took her by the shoulder and guided her out of the ICU waiting room. Out in the hallway, he silently urged her to a door with the word

Private posted in the middle. After opening it, he gestured for her to precede him into a room that was hardly more than a tiny alcove equipped with a small desk, a sink and a light for viewing X-rays.

Nicolette braced herself as he shut the door behind him and turned to her.

"All right," he said quietly. "Here we are. No audience."

From the moment she'd spotted him stepping into the waiting area, her heart had begun to hammer out a tune of hope. But now that the two of them were cocooned together and she was staring at the cool, doubtful expression on his face, her pulse slowed to a fearful crawl.

"I, uh, I suppose you're wondering what I was doing at your house this evening."

Nodding, he silently waited for her to continue.

Nicolette swallowed. "I was—hoping to surprise you. Instead I saw the ambulance driving away and I—" Her head fell forward until she was staring at the tile beneath their feet instead of his stern face. "Oh Ridge, Ridge," she said in a choked voice. "As I raced here to the hospital, I was so afraid. I couldn't bear to imagine my life without you!"

His hand curled around her arm, and with hopeful anticipation, she slowly lifted her head.

"But what about before, Nicci?" he questioned softly. "Before you thought I might be hurt. You were coming to the house to tell me something?"

Stepping forward, she placed her hands on his chest and marveled at the sense of peace she felt at just touching him.

"Yes," she answered as she tilted her head back and looked into his brown eyes. "I wanted to tell you that I love you. That I've been a fool and an even bigger coward for running away from you—from marriage."

Incredible joy swept across his face, and as he pulled her into his arms, Nicolette felt such a thrill of pleasure that her head reeled with it. The scent of him, the hard strength of his body and the warm breath caressing her cheek felt like a delicious drink filling up the empty holes inside her.

"Oh, Nicci, Nicci," he said with a groan against her hair, "I love you so much. I was beginning to think I'd never hear those words from you. What made you change your mind?"

Easing her cheek from the middle of his chest, she looked up at him and smiled through tears of joy. "Mother. She can be a formidable force at times, especially with her children. And let's just say she shook me up pretty good. She made me see how awful it would be to lose you." Nicolette cupped her hands against the sides of his face. "Have I anyway, Ridge? Please tell me I'm not too late. Please tell me that you still want to marry me."

He groaned again, but this time it was a sound of sheer relief. "You're crazy, Nicci, if you think I'd given up on you. Just before Corey's accident I was agonizing over what to do about you—about us. I'd decided I would swallow my pride and try once again to change your mind. I just hadn't figured out yet how I was going to go about doing it." His head shook back and forth with amazement. "Dear God, I never dreamed you'd be coming to me—like this."

His arms tightened around her as though he never intended to let her go, and Nicolette felt the scars inside her blow away like dead leaves tossed into the wind. Ridge truly was a heart mender. He'd made her heart whole again, able to love again.

"I couldn't stay away," she murmured. "These past couple of weeks without you have been utter hell for me, Ridge. And I—" Her head shook with regret as she looked into his eyes. "Well, now I realize that I've handled everything badly. I should have been more open with you from the very start and then maybe—well, maybe you would have understood why I ran from you like a timid little mouse who saw its shadow."

He stroked her hair, and the love she saw in his eyes was such a wondrous sight that she wanted to weep with joy and relief.

"It doesn't matter, Nicci. You don't have to explain."

"Yes," she urgently countered, "I do. I need to tell it all to you. I don't want us to start our life with anything standing in the way. Let me throw this burden away once and for all, Ridge."

Nodding gravely he said, "All right. I'm listening."

Easing out of his arms, she turned her back to him as she tried to pull together the words she needed to say. She didn't know where to begin or how to convey the crushing self-doubt she'd lived with for the past few years. She only knew that she wanted Ridge to see all the fears she'd carried in her heart and why it had made her so hesitant about loving him.

Finally she gathered enough inner strength to face him and speak. "You already know that my marriage to Bill was not an easy one."

He gave her a single nod.

Clenching her hands in a prayerful clasp, Nicolette went on, "You've got to understand that when I married him, I loved him very much. While we were engaged, he was attentive and dedicated to me and appeared to care for me just as much as I did for him. We made plans for the future just like any normal couple does before they walk down the aisle. I had always wanted a family of my own, even more than I'd wanted a medical career. To have a husband and children would be a dream come true for me."

"But it didn't come true," he said grimly.

Pressing fingertips to her drawn forehead, she said, "We were happy at first and I wasn't too disappointed after a couple of years passed and I still hadn't gotten pregnant. Being a P.A. I understood that these things sometimes take time. But then another year slipped by and I started getting anxious, especially when the doctors continued to tell me that they could find nothing that would keep me from conceiving."

Caught by her story now, Ridge's gaze earnestly searched her face. "What was Bill thinking about all this?"

Nicolette's features tightened. "Oh, he played the concerned husband. He tried to reassure me that we'd eventually have children and that I just needed to give it more time. But I was beginning to sense that he wasn't really bothered by the matter. Especially when I suggested we both go for fertility tests and he flatly refused. We had a big row over it and he told me I needed to forget about having babies—that *he* should be enough to make me happy."

"Oh, Nicci, I'm so sorry," he said softly. "You must have felt like he'd deserted you."

Ridge's empathy brought a lump to Nicolette's throat, and she had to look away from him and swallow before she could go on. "Yeah. I realized then that there was a huge gap between us, one that I hadn't even been aware of. When he told me to forget about having children, the joy went out of me, Ridge. I threw myself into my work to forget and maybe even to pretend that everything was right with my marriage. But it wasn't."

To forget. To pretend. Ridge had heard his own mother speak those very words, and suddenly he understood, even more than he had the day of Lillian's visit, how one person could crush the other's spirit until nothing was left.

"So your marriage slid downhill," he said with certainty. "What happened? What finally brought about the divorce?"

She grimaced. "Looking back on it now, I realize I should have gotten out of the marriage earlier, but I kept hoping things would get better, especially if we had a child. I had always considered marriage a sacred vow to God. I didn't want to give up on it— even through bad times. But Bill finally took that choice out of my hands. He asked for a divorce and confessed that while I was working six days a week at the clinic, neglecting him, he'd been using that time to see other women."

"Bastard!" Ridge cursed beneath his breath.

Nicolette sighed. "I called him more than that. Especially when he told me he had plans to marry another woman, one much younger than me, who wasn't married to her job. But the young woman wasn't the biggest hurt Bill hurled at me. He laughingly told me that all the years I'd been trying to conceive a child, he'd been hiding the fact that he'd had a vasectomy."

Ridge stared at her in utter disbelief. "Nicci! No!"

Sarcasm twisted her lips. "Oh, yes. It was

medically impossible for Bill to have children. He'd lied and led me on all those years. I'll never understand why. Why he married me in the first place or stayed with me for nearly nine years. I can only think that it was for my money—Sandbur money—because in the end it was obvious that he didn't love me, and that our goals in life were far, far different."

Ridge was silent for long moments as he digested everything she'd just told him. Wordlessly he reached for her and enveloped her within the tight circle of his arms.

"I wished you'd told me before, when we first met, Nicci," he whispered against her cheek. "I might have understood. Instead, I was asking myself if I'd become tangled up with the same sort of woman who'd broken my heart before. Brittany led me to believe she wanted to be my wife. But when she finally saw that I intended to live the simple life, she left as fast as she could."

Nicolette looked at him with surprise. "You never mentioned that you were engaged before."

"I didn't get as far as giving her a ring. I was headed in that direction, but I guess I was much luckier than you. At least Brittany was honest enough to admit that she couldn't live the sort of life I wanted. That's more than Bill ever was with you." He shook his head with regret. "I feel so awful about all those things I said to you that night you left, Nicci. I wish I could take them all back."

Shaking her head, she tightened her arms around his waist. "We both said awful things. But that's over, Ridge. Now we're going to concentrate on loving each other. If we do that, everything else will fall into place, and our home will fill up with babies. Once that happens, I'm going to cut down on my work so that I can devote myself to our children. And you," she added impishly.

A sexy grin slanted his lips as he turned and quickly locked the door.

His intentions obvious, Nicolette chuckled under her breath. "Don't tell me you're one of *those* kinds of doctors."

With a hungry growl, he snatched her close and brought his lips against hers. "Only with you, my sweet Nicci. Now and forever."

Six weeks later the Sandbur was a picture of merriment. Thousands of clear tiny lights were draped through branches of the oak trees and around the portable dance floor erected in the backyard. The scent of beef smoking slowly over mesquite coals filled the warm night, along with the sounds of a live country band twanging out plenty of Texas two-steps. In addition to the Sandbur's barbecued beef, hundreds of guests were being served from kegs of cold beer and champagne bottles shoved into crushed iced. Loud conversation and laughter competed with the happy sound of music and popping fireworks.

The Fourth of July had already come and gone, but several of the wranglers were out in the open area of the ranch yard setting off firecrackers and Roman candles. After all, the boss lady's daughter had gotten married to her young handsome doctor. It was a time for celebration.

Earlier that evening, Nicolette and Ridge had exchanged vows in the small church he'd attended since moving to Victoria. The building was equipped with only enough pews to handle a few family members and close friends, and the ceremony itself had been quiet and simple, just the way Nicolette and Ridge had wanted it to be.

Barry Macon had driven down from Houston to serve as Ridge's best man, while young Corey had been proud to be a groomsman. Mercedes had miraculously managed to obtain enough leave from her military service to fly over from Diego Garcia to act as maid of honor to her sister. And to Ridge and Nicolette's great surprise, his mother, Lillian, had made the trip to attend her son's wedding and was even planning on staying a few days with Geraldine.

Roses and candles had dressed up the little country church, but it had been Nicolette in her long ivory dress, her face radiant with love, that had made the ceremony beautiful.

Now as hundreds of guests kicked up their heels at the Sandbur reception, Ridge held his wife tightly as the two of them swayed around the dance floor and dreamed of the Hawaiian honeymoon they would be leaving for in just a few short hours.

Some distance from the dance floor, Cordero stood on the patio, silently taking in the merrymaking as he washed down wedding cake with a glass of beer.

Mercedes fondly wrapped her arm around the back of his waist. "First our cousin Raine. Then your brother, Matt. Now my sister, Nicci," she said to her cousin with wry speculation. "The mosquitoes around here must be spreading some sort of love fever. You'd better watch out, Cordero. You might get bitten yourself."

With a mocking laugh, he looked down at her sweet face. "No way! You're the one who caught the bride's bouquet. You're the one who'd better watch out. Some good-looking fly boy might come along and sweep you off your feet."

Mercedes's smile was wan as she lifted a fluted glass to her lips. "I don't believe in that old wedding bouquet tradition."

"Hmm. Well, I don't believe all this marrying has been caused by mosquitoes or potions in the water. Our relatives got married because they wanted to. And I don't want to. So that means I'm safe from the chains of any woman," Cordero said with smiling confidence. "Besides, I'm not going to be around here long enough to catch anything for the next few days. I'm leaving for New Orleans in the morning."

Mercedes's blue eyes turned playful as she studied her cousin's handsome face. "Oh. Is this a trip for business or pleasure?"

His own eyes twinkling, Cordero let out a wicked little chuckle. "Well now, that all depends. I'm delivering Sandbur horses to a buyer. But it's always possible that I could run into a sweet little thing along the way."

Pursing her lips, Mercedes shook her head. "Cordero, are you going to be a rascal the rest of your life?"

Laughing, he grabbed her arm and tugged her toward the dance floor. "Little cousin, I can't think of one thing to stop me."

* * * * *

Don't miss Cordero's story,
HAVING THE COWBOY'S BABY,
Coming in May 2007
from Stella Bagwell
and Silhouette Special Edition.

Turn the page for a sneak preview of
IF I'D NEVER KNOWN YOUR LOVE
by
Georgia Bockoven

From the brand-new series
Harlequin Everlasting Love
Every great love has a story to tell.™

One year, five months and four days missing

There's no way for you to know this, Evan, but I haven't written to you for a few months. Actually, it's been almost a year. I had a hard time picking up a pen once more after we paid the second ransom and then received a letter saying it wasn't enough. I was so sure you were coming home that I took the kids along to Bogotá so they could fly home with you and me, something I swore I'd never do. I've fallen in love with Colombia and the people who've opened their hearts to me. But fear is a constant companion when I'm there. I won't ever expose our children to that kind of danger again.

I'm at a loss over what to do anymore, Evan. I've begged and pleaded and thrown temper tantrums with every official I can corner both here and at home. They've been incredibly tolerant and understanding, but in the end as ineffectual as the rest of us.

I try to imagine what your life is like now, what you do every day, what you're wearing, what you eat. I want to believe that the people who have you are misguided yet kind, that they treat you well. It's how I survive day to day. To think of you being mistreated hurts too much. If I picture you locked away somewhere and suffering, a weight descends on me that makes it almost impossible to get out of bed in the morning.

Your captors surely know you by now. They have to recognize what a good man you are. I imagine you working with their children, telling them that you have children, too, showing them the pictures you carry in your wallet. Can't the men who have you understand how much your children miss you? How can it not matter to them?

How can they keep you away from us all this time? Over and over, we've done what they asked. Are they oblivious to the depth of their cruelty? What kind of people are they that they don't care?

I used to keep a calendar beside our bed next to the peach rose you picked for me before you left. Every night I marked another day, counting how many you'd been gone. I don't do that any longer. I don't want to be reminded of all the days we'll never get back.

When I can't sleep at night, I tell you about my day. I imagine you hearing me and smiling over the details that make up my life now. I never tell you how defeated I feel at moments or how hard I work to hide it from everyone for fear they will see it as a reason to stop believing you are coming home to us.

And I couldn't tell you about the lump I found in my breast and how difficult it was going through all the tests without you here to lean on. The lump was benign—the process reaching that diagnosis utterly terrifying. I couldn't stop thinking about what would happen to Shelly and Jason if something happened to me.

We need you to come home.

I'm worn down with missing you.

I'm going to read this tomorrow and will probably tear it up or burn it in the fireplace. I don't want you to get the idea I ever doubted what I was doing to free you or thought the work a burden. I would gladly spend the rest of my life at it, even if, in the end, we only had one day together.

You are my life, Evan.

I will love you forever.

* * * * *

Don't miss this deeply moving
Harlequin Everlasting Love story
about a woman's struggle
to bring back her
kidnapped husband from Colombia and her
turmoil over whether to let go, finally,
and welcome another man into her life.
IF I'D NEVER KNOWN YOUR LOVE
by Georgia Bockoven
is available March 27, 2007.

And also look for
THE NIGHT WE MET
by Tara Taylor Quinn,
a story about finding love
when you least expect it.

SPECIAL EDITION™

Emotional, compelling stories that capture the intensity of living, loving and creating a family in today's world.

Modern, passionate reads that are powerful and provocative.

nocturne

Dramatic and sensual tales of paranormal romance.

Romances that are sparked by danger and fueled by passion.

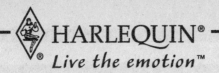
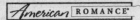

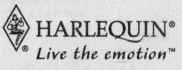